RAINING DEATH

Stone and dust, choking, stinging, pounding into flesh like a horrible hammer blow, filling Prine's eyes, nose, blinding, hurting. He raised himself, painfully, and looked out. He was trapped by the falling rock, pushed aside like a feather before the wind. A dim light came from the lantern he had held, now half buried in dirt and rubble, its flame growing steadily lower.

His gun—where was his gun? He felt for it, straining his dust-filled eyes to see it, but couldn't find it. He half rose again, failed, then tried once more, this time making it to his feet. He stared groggily ahead, somehow not even surprised to see a man standing before him with a .44 leveled at his gut. The Preacher.

"Well, friend, it looks like it's me and you again—and this time I'm going to kill you. . . ."

The Treasure of Jericho Mountain

CAMERON JUDD

BANTAM BOOKS
NEW YORK • TORONTO • LONDON • SYDNEY • AUCKLAND

THE TREASURE OF JERICHO MOUNTAIN

A Bantam Book / published by arrangement with the author

PRINTING HISTORY

Bantam edition / February 1990

ISBN 0-553-28341-3

Published simultaneously in the United States and Canada

Bantam Books are published by Bantam Books, a division of Bantam Doubleday Dell Publishing Group, Inc. Its trademark, consisting of the words "Bantam Books" and the portrayal of a rooster, is Registered in U.S. Patent and Trademark Office and in other countries. Marca Registrada. Bantam Books, 666 Fifth Avenue, New York, New York 10103.

PRINTED IN THE UNITED STATES OF AMERICA

KRI   0 9 8 7 6 5 4 3

To
Matthew Cameron Judd

CHAPTER

1

A town of dust and shadows, of vacant windows and empty doorways. A street of creaking, faded signs and unpainted lumber. This was the corpse of a town, an empty place that knew no life. There had been a time when the streets were living things and the buildings that now stood weather-beaten and empty had housed businesses that thrived and prospered.

Now the town stood empty, a memorial to times that had been and days that would never come again.

Into those dusty streets Jeremy Prine rode, and his eyes were alert and quick as he scanned the rows of ramshackle buildings. For days he had ridden this trail, and there were times when he had been unable to explain to his own satisfaction just why he was doing it. A single, cryptic telegram, a tantalizing message—that had been all that had moved him. When first he received it he had tried to ignore it, but the message, vague though it was, had burned into his mind, stirring feelings that he had long forgotten—the sense of mystery, of adventure.

The first lines had been mere directions to this Colorado ghost town. Then the date and these words: "Important meeting, money to be gained. Arrive before nightfall. Thomas Stuart." That was all. Nothing specific, nothing to hint at what might be involved. But two things about that telegram had drawn his full attention and kept Prine from tossing it aside without a second thought.

Partly it had been the words "money to be gained." Money was one thing he did not possess in abundance right

1

now, and he was interested in anything that might improve his less-than-satisfactory financial condition. There was little work for cowboys these days, especially aging ones. The open range was gone, lined by barbed-wire fences and crisscrossed by railroads. When cattle had been scattered across the range, it had been necessary to round them up, and that required men. Now that cattle ranged within the confines of fenced-in ranges, there was little need for men like Jeremy Prine.

But even more than the money, the thing that had attracted him had been the name on the telegram. Not the entire name—the "Thomas" meant nothing to him—but that last name, the name that called up memories of old friendship, of times good and bad, pleasant and disturbing.

Bob Stuart. Prine whispered the name to himself as his horse sauntered down the dusty and deserted street. How many times had he thought of that name since the days when the conflict between North and South was still raging? He couldn't even begin to estimate; Bob Stuart had been on his mind many times. It was hard to believe that they had lost track of each other; men who suffer together through an ordeal such as the bloody battle at Shiloh should not drift apart. Still, Stuart occupied Prine's thoughts, though now he did not know even if he were living or dead.

Perhaps now he would find out. The odds that the Stuart of the telegram was connected in any way with his old Civil War partner were remote, yet a possibility. At any rate, he would know soon. He had come as the telegram had directed, and if there were anyone else in the town a meeting would be inevitable.

Prine's eyes swept the bare street, looking for some evidence of the presence of another living human being. There was something ghostly about the place, and it filled him with a vague apprehension. He was not one to become frightened at a shadow, and superstition had never plagued him, but the emptiness all around him, combined with the sense of mystery and slight caution the telegram had produced in him, made him realize how essential alertness was right now. He looked carefully from one side of the street to the other, squinting his eyes slightly to look inside the dark interiors of the boarded buildings.

Was that a hoofbeat he heard behind him?

He turned in the saddle, every sense keenly alert. Behind him a shutter banged in the wind, its echo resounding down the street. Prine let out a low sigh and turned forward again.

"Mr. Jeremy Prine, I assume?"

The voice surprised him, causing his hand to drop instinctively to his side arm. Immediately his ears ascertained the direction from which the voice had come, and he saw a slender young man who looked back at him from the porch of a deserted hotel. The fellow had a grin on his face and an almost devilish twinkle in his eye. Prine was struck with the feeling that there was something familiar in the face of the young man, and looked at him intently.

The man was posed casually on the roofed porch, leaning against the supporting post with his arms crossed in front of him and one foot cocked on its toe. He had apparently stepped from the inside of the building just as Prine's attention had been diverted by the loose shutter. He was dressed for riding, but the cut of his clothes was fancy, and even in his dust-coated condition he looked distinguished. His features were well formed and his eyes were brown and clear. He held his pose only a moment, then walked lightly down the steps, his hand extended and his grin unfaded.

"Thomas Stuart, Mr. Prine," he said, his voice light and friendly. "I'm the man who sent you the telegram. I can't tell you how pleased I am that you responded. I've heard a lot about you."

Prine was somewhat at a loss at how to react to this fellow's friendliness. Stuart acted as if he had known him for years, though Prine could not recall where they might have met. The feeling that the young man's face was familiar continued, though. Prine felt slightly on the defensive.

The feeling of recognition only grew as Prine shook the extended hand.

"Mr. Stuart, who is your father?" Prine's words seldom failed to come straight to the point.

Stuart grinned. "So you've got it figured out already,

have you? My father is—or was—Robert Stuart, the very one who you served with in the Confederate Army. It was through him that I heard of you."

Prine shook the man's hand again when he heard that, but a shiver of sadness rose up in him. "You say he *was* your father—I guess that means old Bob's dead, doesn't it?"

Stuart nodded. "I'm sorry to have to bring you the news. From what Father said I gathered you two were pretty close back in the war."

Prine dismounted. "We were. Those weren't good times, by any means, but it was a time of good friendships."

Prine began walking his mount toward the deserted livery stable down the street. "I truly do hate to hear that old Bob's dead—I truly do. What of your ma, Mr. Stuart?"

"She's gone too, a year after Father. After he died I don't think she cared to live anymore. He left her a lot as far as material things go—money, a good home—but it wasn't the things he could give her that meant much to Ma—it was Father himself. I did my best for her after he died, but I couldn't take his place. She followed on right after him, and in a way I think that's just what she wanted to do."

Prine unsaddled his gelding in the shadows of the livery, putting the animal in one of the empty stalls. What remnants of hay that lay around on the floor were so old and dry as to be useless, but in a rain barrel outside there was water. Prine found an old battered bucket and filled it, setting it before the horse. The only other animal in the building was a stallion, Stuart's mount.

Prine pulled a cloth tobacco sack from his vest pocket and poked it toward Stuart with a faint grunt. The other refused the offer politely, and Prine paused long enough to expertly roll a cigarette with experienced fingers. He lit it and drew in a huge cloud of fragrant smoke with a look of satisfaction on his face. The pair walked out of the livery into the light of the street.

Stuart led the way back to the hotel. "I brought a bottle of rye. Can I interest you in a drink?"

That was the best offer Prine had received in some time, and he told Stuart as much. Already he was beginning to like the young fellow in spite of his natural apprehensions, partly because he was Bob Stuart's son, and partly because of some unidentifiable something in his pleasant disposition and disarming smile. But Prine also wondered if maybe he were letting down his guard a bit too early. After all, he didn't even know what this man had in mind.

The interior of the old hotel lobby was like a faded photograph, a dusty relic. The furniture was still there, sitting as if the occupants had decided in one moment to walk out the door and never return. Dust coated the room, half an inch thick in some places, collected over a decade and undisturbed by cloth or broom. A few clean spots betrayed the areas where Stuart had been waiting. Prine wondered how long the young man had been there.

Stuart disappeared behind a counter and reappeared with a bottle of rye whiskey. He popped the cork and filled two small glasses he had pulled from somewhere beneath the counter. Prine took his drink and drained a large swallow.

"The telegram mentioned a meeting. Is this it?"

"You might say this is the waiting period. There are still others to come." Stuart sipped his drink slowly and smiled. "I think you will be surprised—and pleased—when you see who they are."

Prine was intrigued. It was a tantalizing mystery, this strange man and his ghost-town meeting. But one mystery had been solved: the question of why Prine felt the fellow was familiar. It was because in the smile and crinkle of the young man's eyes he saw a reflection of the Stuart he had fought beside years before. The younger Stuart was in many ways the image of his father. It made Prine feel a little nostalgic to look at him, and reminded him also of how many years had passed since he was this man's age. It made him feel rather ancient.

Stuart looked at Prine's face and read the question there. He flashed his self-confident smile again. "I'm sure you're wondering what this is all about. Before I fill you in, let me assure you that if you listen to what I propose, then act on it, you stand to make a good deal of money."

At that moment the neighing of a horse punctuated

Stuart's words, and Prine's eyes flashed toward the open door to the street beyond.

"Ah!" exclaimed Stuart. "I think more of our party have arrived."

It took Prine only an instant to recognize the bearded, gruff-looking man who rode down the street. The younger man by his side he couldn't place.

"John Ballard! You old devil! Who would have thought . . ." Prine's excitement got the best of his common sense, and he ran out into the street, giving his greeting with such vigor that the approaching riders' horses nearly reared beneath them. The bearded man sent forth a low curse and went for his gun, simultaneously trying to still his agitated mount. The younger man was so startled that he came close to losing his seat in the saddle, even without the help of his startled gelding.

John Ballard's gun was halfway out of its holster before he recognized the figure before him. His eyes changed. A softness came onto his features.

"Prine? Jeremy Prine?" The gun went back into its holster. The horse quieted, and the bearded man stared openmouthed at Prine. The younger man had more trouble controlling his animal, but when finally he succeeded he looked first at Prine, then at the bearded man, with an expression of confusion.

In a moment Ballard was out of his saddle and clasping the hand of Prine. Both men were smiling broadly, almost ridiculously, hands pumping and friendly arms clasping each other's shoulders. This was a reunion that neither was expecting but which both found intensely pleasant. Stuart stood watching upon the porch, the pose in which Prine had first seen him resumed, and a smile warmed his features. But unnoticed by the others, his expression grew colder when he glanced toward the young man who had ridden in beside Ballard. He glared at him silently.

"You old swamp rat!" Prine exclaimed, his grin still beaming. "I would never have imagined that I would see you here! I can't tell you how many times I've thought about you since the old days."

"Same with me, Prine! I figured I would probably never see you again. Oh, I planned to look you up a few years after the war was over, but you know how those things work out." He stopped and looked at his friend, as if the mere sight of him gave him immense satisfaction. "Jeremy Prine! Alive and kicking, and here in the flesh! I guess all the old Confederacy isn't gone, after all!"

"Ballard, that wouldn't be your boy there, would it? It seems I see a little of your good looks in his face."

Ballard grinned and glanced at the mounted young man. "That's my only boy, Prine, and I'm right proud of him. I didn't aim to come here without him by my side. Thad, get down here! I want you to meet an old war partner of mine—Lord knows you've heard enough tales about him! Come on, boy!"

The tag "boy" didn't fit the man; he was at least two or three years past twenty, every bit as old as Stuart, and very muscled. He dismounted expertly, then walked with a firm stride to where Prine and his father stood. His hand came out and Prine grasped it. The grip was strong.

"Pleased to meet you, Mr. Prine. Father's told me a lot of tales about you and the rest of that wartime gang you all hung around with."

Prine grinned. "You can drop the 'Mr.'—Prine will be sufficient. It looks like old Ballard's got a good one to carry on after him. I'm proud to meet you."

"Well, it seems this reunion is more pleasant than I expected! It makes me proud that I brought you together."

The voice was Stuart's. Prine had almost forgotten the man's presence. Ballard eyed the young fellow strangely, as did Thad, but the pleasant grin remained on Stuart's face as he introduced himself to the newcomers.

Ballard's handshake was a good deal less spirited than it had been with Prine. His gaze left no doubt that he was wary. Prine expected that. Ballard had always been a cautious man in the earlier years, and the fact that he had not come on this journey alone was sufficient proof he had not changed.

But when Ballard learned the identity of Stuart's father, he softened a good deal and his attitude became more open. And when Stuart offered the new arrivals a drink of rye, Ballard was almost totally converted. After seeing to the horses, he headed up the steps to the hotel in high spirits, with Thad close behind.

The quartet passed several long and pleasant minutes sipping whiskey and discussing bygone times before any serious conversation began. Prine had much he wished to hear from his old friend, and Ballard was every bit as curious about Prine's affairs. He was curious, too, about Bob Stuart, and he was saddened visibly when the younger Stuart related the same fact he had told Prine. Ballard looked down into his near-empty shot glass and sighed.

"It gets us all sooner or later. I hate to hear that old Bob's gone—I dearly would have liked to see him again."

When Prine asked Ballard about his activities since the war, the bearded man brightened and leaned back in his chair as he talked.

"After the war I headed down into Georgia for a while, but things were bad there. The war had pretty much demolished the land . . . there were homes burned, farms destroyed, just general ruin all over. I didn't stay long— there was no good way for a free-roaming man like me to make an honest living. I headed across the Mississippi, roamed a while. I wound up in Missouri and started farming for a feller. Pretty soon I had saved enough to buy a little land for myself, and I began farming on my own. Got married, had Thad here, and that's pretty much how it went. I never got rich, but then I never starved neither. My wife, she's gone now—it's been five, six years—but me and old Thad are still there, making a go of it. I guess I should be there tending to my business right now, but that telegram got my curiosity up and I had to find out what it was about." He eyed Stuart with open curiosity.

Prine told his own story then. "I never tried farming like you did, Ballard—couldn't ever stand to stomp through hog manure and get dirt underneath my fingernails any more than I had to. But after the war there wasn't nothing left for me, neither. I came to Kansas, then hit Montana as a cowboy. It was a good life for a while, but now there's just not much call for an over-the-hill cowpoke. Barbed wire and railroads have just about knocked men like me out of business. I've been riding the soup line for some time now, working at whatever kind of job I can pick up. It don't sound like much, but I guess in a way it suits me. I'm awful short on funds about now, but I reckon I'll live. 'Specially if Mr. Stuart's proposition is as good as he makes it sound."

He glanced over at the young man, who sat casually sipping his drink. After the pause grew sufficiently long for Stuart to tell that the reminiscences were over, he set the drink down with a rather dramatic motion and looked closely at each of the men.

"Well, gentlemen, I can see that you're ready to discuss the reason I called you here. I hesitate to do it just jet, though, for what I have to tell you is rather long and detailed, and there is one person yet to arrive. Do you have the patience to wait a while longer?"

"Just who are you expecting?" Ballard asked.

"Another of your war partners," he returned. "Silas Kent."

Ballard's expression was unchanged as he stated bluntly, "Kent is dead. He was killed in a Kentucky coal-mining accident two years ago. I got word through some kin of mine that knew him."

Stuart showed disappointment, but brightened quickly. "In that case we can begin," he said. But then he stopped, and he looked as if he were struggling for words to say something that he found unpleasant and difficult. He glanced briefly at Thad Ballard.

"Gentlemen," he began at length, "I have no wish to offend anyone in this room. But, Mr. Ballard, there is something I must say. The proposition I have to discuss with you is of a unique nature, and you already realize from the telegram that money is involved." He paused, looking uncomfortable. "Mr. Prine and Mr. Ballard, I chose you because I knew from my father that you were men of absolute trustworthiness. Only because of your reputations are you here. It should be clear not only from the sketchy nature of the telegram, but also from this isolated meeting place, that this is a highly secretive affair. What I'm getting at, Mr. Ballard, is that—no offense intended—I hadn't counted on any of you bringing anyone with you. You must understand, I have to be totally certain that I can trust—"

Ballard seemed to grow taller in his seat, and his face became a thunderstorm of anger, his expression clouding and his eyes flashing lightning. His bearing was sufficient to halt Stuart's words in midsentence, and every eye turned on Ballard in anticipation of an outburst of fury.

Ballard stood, his hulking form rising to its full height, well over six feet. Thad looked humble, quiet. It was obvious that he had seen his father like this many times before and knew what was coming. Prine had seen it before, too, and waited expectantly for the bear to roar.

"Stuart, I am a man of family pride. Thad here is a Ballard. He's had honesty beat into him since the day he was born. Anywhere I go he goes—it's always been like that and it ain't about to change. After that no more need be said."

Ballard sat down again, glaring rather haughtily. Stuart returned Ballard's stare unflinchingly, in spite of the tirade to which he had been subjected. Prine sat to the side, trying to hide the grin that kept creeping onto his face. It had been a long time since he had seen John Ballard raging and it was good to see.

Stuart's words were crisp and articulate, delivered with biting politeness. "Sir, were you to understand the nature of what I have to discuss you would see clearly the need for discretion this affair warrants. Do not take my doubts as an insult to your family. I have interests to protect, and I intend to do it. I have no doubt that you have raised your son well. I will take your word that he will betray no secrets nor act in his own self-interest at the expense of the rest of us. Silas Kent is dead—your son shall replace him in this party. Is that sufficient to satisfy your 'family pride,' Mr. Ballard?" Prine had never seen a man strut while sitting down, but Stuart had almost accomplished it.

The fire in Ballard's eyes had cooled slightly, and his only answer was a grunt that Stuart took as an affirmative reply. He looked slowly from one man to another, as if waiting for comment. Receiving none, he began to speak.

"Very well, then. But let us all understand that each of us, myself included, will act as gentlemen at all times. Once you hear what I have to say I think you will be glad you made this trip.

"But there is one thing that I must trust from each of you: absolute silence to anyone else about what I am going to reveal. Once I share with you the information I possess, I shall be, in a manner of speaking, at your mercy. I have called you here because I am totally convinced of your honesty. But can I have your word of honor that, whether you consent to my proposal or not, you will remain absolutely silent about anything I am about to reveal, and that you will hold in confidence anything I say?" He looked into faces that had become cold sober and intent.

Prine spoke first. "You have my word, Mr. Stuart."

"And mine." Ballard's words were low and gruff.

Stuart nodded, then looked at the last member of the party. Thad Ballard stared at him briefly, then nodded his head.

Stuart breathed deeply, as if in preparation for a statement of great import. He reached inside his vest and came out with an oilskin packet bound tightly with cords. He dropped it on the table with a dramatic gesture.

"Gentlemen, within that packet lies information that could make each of us a great deal of money."

CHAPTER

3

Ballard leaned forward, eyes shining.

"What are you talking about?"

"About money, Mr. Ballard. Honest money, and plenty of it."

"How much?"

"Fifty thousand dollars to divide between us."

Thad whistled and glanced at Prine, who lifted his brows.

"That's a lot," Ballard said. "Especially to come by honestly. What's in that packet?"

"Perhaps the best way to answer that is to tell you a story, one that leads up to where we are right now. It has to do with my father and an old outlaw named Wesley Stoner."

"I've heard of him," Thad said. "Robbed a lot of stages and trains back during the war."

"Yes," Stuart said. "And right after the war is where my story begins. Mr. Prine, Father never roamed like you did after the fighting ended; he headed back to Virginia and settled back into life on our old farm. The war had left it relatively untouched, which was both amazing and fortunate. Father became prosperous relatively quickly. He was able to buy out smaller farms around his, and in a few years he had a spread of land to rival some of the Southern plantations before the war.

"Father used to ride the grounds of the farm, partly to keep up with crops and herds, partly because he enjoyed it. Many times he would find small jobs to be done and do

13

them himself, which made him come home late. Mother was used to that and didn't worry about it much.

"But on one particular August evening shortly before he died, Father was making his rounds when he heard a groan come from a woods alongside the road. He investigated and found a man propped up against a tree. He didn't recognize him. The fellow was mortally wounded, though; that Father could tell right away. Father was on horseback and had no wagon to haul the man in, so there was little he could do immediately except try to comfort and settle him and promise to go for help as quickly as he could.

"But the man wouldn't let Father go; he wanted to talk. He said he had been robbed along a public road nearby by some highwaymen who had taken his cash and watch. The man had crawled back into the woods to escape them. He moaned on about it being a punishment for his past sins, or something like that. Father thought the fellow was going out of his head from his wounds.

"The man said he had been traveling toward Washington to repay an old debt to the government. He talked about papers sewn into the lining of his coat. These were important and secret, he said, and related to what he was doing.

"Father was skeptical, and asked the man why he would tell something like that to a stranger, if it were true. The man said that Father obviously had been divinely sent to him to finish the job he couldn't. Then he sang a line or two from a hymn, and Father was certain he was insane.

"I came by in a wagon about this time; I had been visiting a lady friend who lived a few miles away. I heard the man singing, and Father's voice, and found them in the woods. Father and I got the man onto the wagon and raced for the house, afraid he would die before we got him there.

"But he lived. Father sent a servant for a doctor, and we carried the man inside and tried to make him as comfortable as we could while we waited. Mother brought the man some wine, which seemed to relax him some. He began talking again.

"He claimed he was Wesley Stoner, the old outlaw, and that he was on his way to the capital to reveal the location of a federal gold shipment he and some cohorts had stolen years before. Some of the gold they had converted to cash and spent, he said. But the rest, Stoner told us, he had managed to get away from the rest and hide somewhere where it would never be found. Then he had successfully set about to murder his old companions to make sure they never got their hands on the gold again.

"Then something most unexpected happened to Stoner. He underwent a religious conversion, apparently a very sincere and thorough one. He put himself upon a quest to return what he had stolen and then give himself up to the federal government for whatever punishment they saw fit for him. He wrote a detailed description of where the gold was hidden and began his journey. He was nearing the end of it when he was robbed near our farm.

"He passed out when he finished his story, and though Father and I were bursting with questions, it was no use. He never woke up again. Without speaking of it, Father and I took his coat and hid it. The doctor arrived and pronounced the man dead, and later an undertaker carted him off. When we were alone, Father and I ripped out the lining of his coat. It was just as he had said—the directions were there. Now they are in the packet that you see lying before us.

"Father was excited by the whole affair, especially when some research revealed that a reward of $50,000 had been offered by the government shortly after the theft of the gold. We researched further and found the reward offer had never been terminated. You knew Father as well as I did—you know he would not keep stolen gold. But the reward was another thing entirely.

"Father and I checked and rechecked Stoner's story and found it plausible. We planned then to take over Stoner's quest, but with a different approach. Rather than simply give the government directions to where the gold was hidden, we would actually recover it ourselves and bring it in for the reward. But then Father took ill. A few weeks later he was dead.

"It was he who suggested to me that I contact you men to carry this thing through. You were the only men he knew, he said, who could be counted on to be thoroughly honest. And by the time Father fell ill, a situation had

developed that we knew would require good and capable
men to deal with. More about that in a moment. So I
promised him that contact you I would . . . and I have.

"And that, my friends, is why I have called you here,
and what I propose to do. I want you to help me recover
that gold and get it into the proper hands, and we will
divide the reward among ourselves."

Stuart stopped speaking, and for a time there was only
silence.

"Well, it figures that old Bob would think of us, Prine.
That always was his way," Ballard said.

Stuart looked at them intently. "There is more you
have to know," he said. "Danger isn't merely a possibility in
this venture—it's a certainty. Word of Stoner's quest apparently had leaked to people who should not have heard of it,
and I think they suspect I have the packet. You should
understand that this could be a deadly business. That's what
I meant when I said the situation called for capable men. If
there was no danger, I could simply go recover the gold
myself." He paused. "Now I suppose it's up to you."

The time for decision had come, and the three men
who would have to make it became silent again. The wind
whistled around the eaves of the old hotel building. Finally
Ballard spoke out.

"Stuart, count me in. I guess I feel like this one is for
old Bob."

"If my father is involved, then I'm involved," Thad
quickly said.

All eyes turned to Prine. He grinned, shrugged, and
said, "I reckon I'm too impoverished to say no. Besides, it's
like Ballard said: This one's for Bob."

Stuart smiled broadly. "Friends, I think this calls for a
drink."

Together the four men toasted the coming adventure.
Stuart, with his big grin, looked more than ever like his late
father.

Ballard drained his drink and slammed down the glass
with a bang. "Well, Stuart, where's that gold?"

Stuart opened his packet. He pulled out a crumpled
piece of brown paper covered with scrawled writing, and

another upon which was drawn a map. Stuart held up the hand-scrawled sheet.

"This is Stoner's description of where the gold is hidden. It's three, three and a half days' ride from here. Have you heard of the old mining town of Jericho Creek? Above it stands Jericho Mountain. That's where we'll find what we're after. It should be relatively easy to get—if we can hold off the others after it."

"And who are they?" Prine asked.

"I told you about Stoner having his old partners murdered. One thing he didn't take into consideration was their families. The daughter of one of his old partners, name of Tate, discovered Stoner was behind her father's death and learned about the gold. After Stoner died, Father and I quietly made some inquiries to make sure his story held together. But we were not quiet enough, apparently, for somehow Tate's daughter—Priscilla is her name—discovered we had the information. I think she has pulled together a group of gunmen to track me down and get it. I have seen evidence recently that I'm being followed, by the way."

Ballard looked concerned. "Followed here?"

"I don't think so. I think I threw them off. Let's just hope nobody followed *you* for any reason."

The thought was slightly unnerving. The men pondered it a moment. Prine stood. "I suggest we get some sleep," he said. "I figure you're planning on a first-light pullout, Stuart?"

"I am."

The others stood. "The horses will need some grazing," Thad said. "There's an old fenced-in grassy graveyard on the far edge of town. I'll put them there."

"I'll lend a hand," Prine said.

The two walked out into the dusky evening. In the fading light, the old town seemed even more ghostly than before.

"This place is downright scary," Thad commented. "Puts a man on edge."

They got the horses and let them to the cemetery at the other end of the street. Beside the graveyard stood a small, crumbling church house. They worked open the rusty gate and turned the horses into the fenced lot.

"That ought to hold them," Prine said.

They returned to the hotel and found that Stuart and Ballard had brought in the saddlebags and bedrolls. Ballard already was spreading his roll. Stuart was standing beside the dusty window, looking out at the gathering night.

Ballard had just started to pull off his boots when they heard noise from the horses at the graveyard. Prine wheeled, drew his pistol, and went to the door. Ballard pulled on his boots and joined him.

"Somebody's down there," Prine said.

Ballard pushed past him and onto the porch. He stomped heavily down the porch steps to the street, his pistol out.

Down the street a rifle cracked and a bullet slammed one of the porch columns behind Ballard, who swore and ran to the other side of the street. He dropped behind the end of a short stretch of boardwalk.

Prine and Thad exited the hotel, hugging the front wall, and ducked into an adjacent alley. They glanced at Ballard, who returned the look with a flashing eye. He was all right.

Stuart appeared. He drew another shot from near the graveyard; dirt blasted upward behind his heels. He backed against the wall.

"This thing we've gotten into might be a little more difficult than I anticipated," Prine said.

CHAPTER

4

Prine could just see about half the cemetery where the horses were fenced. They were still there, nervous and frightened by the gunfire—but the important thing was they were there.

Prine strained, through the thickening dusk, to catch some glimpse of movement that might indicate where the gunmen were hidden. He knew their approximate location, but the twilight masked their hiding place and made it impossible to get off a shot at them with any hope of accuracy. The only good thing about it was that the gunmen were having the same difficulty.

For a time there was little sound from either end of the street. Everyone was waiting, trying to determine the location of the enemy. Prine wondered if their attackers were part of the gang led by the girl Stuart had talked about.

Something moved across the street; it was Ballard, creeping slowly in the shadows up to parallel Prine. Thad saw his father and quietly darted across the weedy dirt street. From the area of the church and graveyard came three blasts of gunfire—but Thad made it safely to his father's side.

More silence. Prine looked over at Ballard and Thad, trying to communicate with them silently. Ballard looked back at him closely; the men tried to read gestures and expressions as best the light would allow. Somehow their silent communication came through, for they began moving together, very slowly, up the street, hugging the walls and shadowed places.

Prine noticed Stuart was gone, then almost immediately detected motion atop a building just down from him. He started and lifted his pistol, then saw Stuart's shoulders and head limned against the still-glowing, indigo sky. Stuart glanced down at him, lifting a thumb to indicate he was there for a reason. Prine thumbed back at him, then glanced across at Ballard and Thad—only to find Thad too was now gone.

He stopped a moment, wondering what had happened. But then Ballard gave him a thumbs-up and laid an upright finger over his lips. Prine nodded and waited. In a few moments he heard someone else scramble onto the building just ahead; another form joined Stuart's atop the structure. Thad had recrossed the street far enough back to not be seen by the graveyard gunmen, and had climbed onto the roof with Stuart.

Motion at the graveyard—then Ballard's pistol roared and spat fire. Prine, distracted, had not seen what Ballard had: One of the gunmen had darted from the graveyard toward a recessed door on the same side of the street as Prine, and about forty-five degrees across from where Ballard was. Because of the recess Prine could not shoot at the man, and because of the man's location Ballard was now hampered from further advance.

Prine, hugging the wall, leaned out a bit to try to get perspective, and the man in the recessed doorway suddenly leaned out as well and fired. Prine was almost hit; he pulled back flat against the unpainted board wall.

He didn't want to take any more that close. Prine leaned out again, fired two quick shots to make sure the gunman stayed within his recess, and tried to move forward. But gunfire came from the graveyard at the same time, forcing Prine back. Prine might have taken a bullet had not Ballard joined fire then, quieting the blasts from the graveyard.

Prine realized now how perilous was Ballard's position, as well as his. The only hope was to get the man out of that doorway ahead, or Ballard would be bound to take a bullet sooner or later.

Suddenly Stuart and Thad fired simultaneous shots from the roof toward the graveyard, apparently having detected movement down that way. Prine both welcomed and feared the shots. It would be easy to kill the horses down there, shooting at mere movements. But in the darkness there was little else to do.

In any case, the gunfire from above gave Prine his opportunity to move. He launched out, straight forward, then into an alley. There he stopped for a second, took a breath, and headed on toward the rear of the row of buildings.

He counted buildings as he moved along, looking for the one with the recessed door in which the gunman hid. He hoped there would be an open back way into the building so he could surprise the man from the rear. Reaching the building, though, he found the back doorway boarded up.

But there was also a window, and it was not boarded. Two or three of the panes were broken out. Prine hunkered down and sneaked forward to a spot just below the window, then carefully rose to peer over the edge of the rotting sill.

The darkness inside the structure was dense. But as Prine's eyes adjusted he began to make out a faint rectangle of light at the front end of the building. The front doorway, mostly glass—and in it the silhouetted black form of the gunman. Prine grinned.

He put the barrel of his pistol through one of the broken panes and carefully sighted. When he had the man locked in, he whistled. The man heard it, spun, and Prine fired.

The glass in the front door shattered as the man jerked and staggered back into the street. Prine heard gunfire from Thad and Stuart's roof, as well as from Ballard's spot, and the man collapsed, punctured with multiple shots.

Then came Thad's voice: "Your partner's dead! Give it up and come out, and we'll let you live!"

Prine smiled and nodded. An intelligent fellow, that Thad. Just like his father. He knew it would be worthwhile to take the other gunman alive. Prine was sure that one gunman was all that remained; there had been no evidence of any more than two men. Prine wondered if the gunmen had attacked randomly, or if they were after Stuart's packet. He suspected the latter. Why would two men take on four unless driven by the strongest motivation? In Prine's experience, only two things had the ability to inspire that level of motivation: women and wealth.

Prine headed farther down the row of buildings to the end. The church house stood around the corner, diagonally from him and almost all the way across the street. The graveyard was on the side of the church that faced Prine. Keeping himself hidden behind the last building in the row, Prine carefully peered around the back corner.

He saw a man, crouched behind a big stump. The man was aiming, apparently at Thad and Stuart. He fired off a shot that went high. Prine could tell the gunman was scared; he wasn't shooting well.

Suddenly Prine was startled, but then began to grin. He had seen a big shadow, like a bear, emerging from the darkness behind the remaining gunman. Prine would know that shape anywhere—Ballard. Obviously Ballard wanted this man alive, too, for if he had wanted to kill him he could have done so at any time since he had crept around behind him.

"Drop it," Prine heard Ballard say.

The gunman, startled, leapt up and dropped his pistol. He raised his hands high in the air. Prine grinned more broadly and holstered his own pistol. He stepped out.

"Good job, Ballard. You ain't lost the touch, that I can see."

Ballard was about to answer when a rifle fired on Thad and Stuart's rooftop perch, and the surrendering gunman shuddered and fell. Ballard swore and went to him; Prine was with him in another half second. Ballard felt the neck for a pulse, then shook his head and swore again. Suddenly Ballard stood.

"Thad! Was that you who killed this man?"

Thad's voice called back: "No sir. It was Stuart."

"Stuart, you fool, didn't you see he had given up?" Prine yelled.

"I certainly didn't. It looked to me like he was about to kill Ballard," Stuart shouted back.

"Then you're a blind man," Prine spat in return.

In a few moments Thad and Stuart had descended from the roof and stood with Prine and Ballard beside the bodies, which now had been dragged together. Stuart looked upset. "I'm sorry," he said. "If I had realized you had him under control, I wouldn't have killed him. I simply couldn't see that well from where I was."

"That's a funny thing, then," Ballard returned. "You surely saw well enough to put a bullet between his shoulder blades at a dern long range!"

"A lucky shot," Stuart said.

"Unlucky is more like it," Prine responded. "We could have quizzed this man for information, found out if he and his partner were working alone or with that Tate female you talked about."

"I understand. I'm sorry," Stuart said. He looked sincerely repentant.

"Well, ain't no point in jawing over what can't be changed," Ballard said. "At least we still got the horses. Maybe that's all they were after—stealing our horses. Maybe they didn't know about the packet."

"I don't buy that," Prine said. "You ever seen two men who would fight as hard as these did just for the kind of wore-out nags we're riding?"

Ballard eyed his old partner silently, seeing his point. For a time everyone was silent, thinking it over.

"Perhaps we should ride out at once," Stuart suggested.

"Perhaps we should at that," Prine said. "There's a trading post and little settlement north of here a few miles. I suggest we make for it. We got moon to ride by and a trail we can see."

"What should we do with these men?" Thad asked.

"Leave them. If there's any more about here who are after the packet, our shooting might have drawn them. And I, for one, have no desire to become the newest dead thing in this dead town."

"Thad, let's go for the saddles," Ballard said.

CHAPTER

5

There was little talk as the group tensely saddled the horses. Silently they rode, every sense alert and every hand ready to drop to the butt of a pistol at a moment's notice. Ballard rode in the lead, followed by Thad, and close behind him was Stuart. Prine brought up the rear, aware that his position was particularly strategic, for if there were other men who sought after the packet, it was likely that they would approach from behind. Prine was very conscious of how good a target his back would make for anyone who managed to approach unheard from the rear. It sent a tingle through his skin.

For two hours they rode, the trail nearly invisible in the darkness. On either side the forest was dark and frightening. At almost any point they could be bushwhacked with scarcely a warning.

When Ballard reached a clearer spot on the trail, the moonlight streaming through the branches above him, he turned, guiding his horse into a small gap in the brush to the left of the trail. The others followed; no one questioned Ballard's move. Prine knew what the husky man was doing—his sharp eye had spotted a good spot for camping somewhere off the trail, someplace that would hide them and at the same time give them a fairly clear view of the woods around them, at least as much as the dim moonlight would allow. Prine had always envied Ballard for his catlike ability to see in the darkness.

They dismounted, hobbling their horses in a patch of

24

coarse forest grass. The sound of a nearby bubbling spring reached them. Ballard had chosen an excellent campsite.

The conversation was scant as the group cleared the ground and laid out bedrolls. Thad took first watch, and throughout the remainder of the night the men alternated at sentry duty. When the sun at last filtered through the trees the next morning, casting a green glow upon the camp, all of the men were rested.

They dined on jerky and water from the spring. They didn't have an abundance of food, only what each had brought for himself. Ballard grumbled because of the lack of coffee, but he knew as well as any of them that building a fire would be dangerous.

They had found and brought with them the horses of the men they had fought, eliminating the need to buy pack mules and also giving them a chance to switch mounts and rest their own horses. Prine now rode on a big dun, a strong animal, though more unruly than his usual mount. Stuart rode the smaller dun that they had inherited from the men they had battled.

After an hour's ride the trail was wider, the trees thinner, and the woods filled with grasses and saplings. There was less tension amid the group, and Prine allowed himself the luxury of whistling beneath his breath. Still, though, he found himself continually glancing over his shoulder.

They reached the trading post at noon sharp. The sun was hot, beaming directly above, and there were not many trees to shade them. The post was a low, squatty, ugly place with a smattering of houses and businesses nearby.

They ate a poor dinner in the post's cafe, and at last Ballard got his coffee. They were alone, seated around a large table and saying little, but Prine fancied that the man behind the bar gave them a searching look. He wondered if perhaps the fellow knew something about who they were, maybe even what they were carrying. He hoped not. If the packet were that well known, then there would be more threat than just the Tate gang.

They paid their bill and stepped out into the street. The light was almost blinding after the darkness of the cafe.

"Let's you and me go after some supplies," Ballard said to Prine.

"You want us to go with you?"

"No, Thad. You and Stuart stay here and look after the horses. The less show we can make out of this the better."

Ballard and Prine walked across to a shabby building with a faded sign that read DRY GOODS, GROCERIES, HARDWARE. The interior was dark and cool, and smelled of dust that had not been swept out since the year before.

"Pick and shovel? I got plenty of both, right in the back." The keeper looked as grubby as his store. He leaned across the counter smoking a cigar and watching the two men with strange interest.

Ballard picked the best of the tools the store carried and moved them to the counter. Prine had already gathered foodstuffs and other supplies. Ballard pulled a small roll of bills from his pocket and paid the storekeeper. The man handed him his change, puffing the cigar through yellow teeth.

"You men from around here?"

"Why do you ask?"

"No reason. Just nosy, I guess." Then he looked at them as if he were sizing them up, the cigar sending out a steady flow of strong-smelling smoke. He spoke again.

"There was a good-sized group of men in here yesterday asking if any others had come through lately," he said. "I told 'em no. Think they might be looking for you?"

Ballard shot Prine a quick glance. "I don't reckon so. Did you know any of them?" Ballard asked the question a bit too quickly. The grubby storekeeper noticed, but he said nothing of it.

"Nope. Never seen any of 'em before. I tell you one thing, though—they were sure a rough-looking bunch. Not the kind that I like to deal with." He handed the tools across to Ballard. "You be careful. I don't know you from Adam, nor what your business is, but that group might have been highwaymen looking for easy victims. Pardon me if I've got into your private business a little—I just thought you deserved fair warning."

Prine looked the fellow over. He seemed trustworthy.

"'Preciate it."

He and Ballard moved on out the door and onto the porch. The man called to them from inside.

"There was something unusual about that bunch."

"What was that?"

"Had a girl with 'em—pretty and blond. She seemed to be part of them."

Ballard and Prine both knew full well the significance of that.

From Ballard's fast stride Prine could tell he was nervous. He didn't blame him.

They walked back over to where Thad and Stuart waited. The two young men appeared restless and uncomfortable.

"Let's get out of here," Thad said as the men approached. "We've been getting some strange looks. I don't like it."

"Neither do I, Thad," said Prine. Quickly he related what the storekeeper had told them. Stuart grew agitated.

"They really are looking for me, then," he said. "Let's go."

The storekeeper stood on the porch of his store, still puffing his cigar and watching the leaving riders. They rode with their backs toward him, disappearing into the woods just beyond the outskirts of town. He stayed there for a while longer, then turned and walked back into his store.

CHAPTER

6

The land cleared and widened, giving a good view in all directions. This was big land, open land, the kind that had always made Prine feel glad to be on the move.

But today he felt differently about it. There was danger from the rear; he sensed it, as surely as if a band of armed riders were galloping up within full view. In a paradoxical way Prine almost wanted some sort of attack to come, just to relieve the tension of expectation. It would be better to fight openly than to ride and wonder how many and how strong the enemy was.

Prine was in the rear again. An almost military order had set itself up in the group with no conscious design by any of them. Ballard rode in the lead, and his instincts were trusted by every member of the party. Stuart rode in the middle, accompanied by Thad. Prine followed, riding with ears listening for any surprises from behind.

Prine said nothing of his apprehensions to the rest of the group. Probably Ballard felt the same thing already.

All day they rode, hardly stopping, except to spell the horses and take a smoke beside the road. They made good time, for the travel was steady and the trail was well worn.

When the sun began westering, Ballard started searching for a campsite. Before them was another stretch of woods. Into it they rode. The trail wound beneath the dark trees.

Ballard located a clearing and there they stopped. The sunlight was not entirely gone, but the forest was darker than open land.

It was a cold supper again. Prine sat beside Ballard as he ate and spoke privately to the man.

"We're being followed."

"I know it. I've known it all day. I expect whoever it is will try something tonight."

"I never saw nobody, so I can't figure out how many there are. Could be anywhere from just a couple to the whole Tate gang. Somehow I think it isn't the gang, though. That storekeeper said they were there yesterday, so that should put 'em somewhere ahead of us."

"They could have doubled back. I figure we'll find out tonight."

The pair agreed that Thad and Stuart had best be warned, so they told them of their suspicions, and were mildly surprised when the two younger men told them they had felt the same way all day.

"We figure they'll try to take us in our sleep tonight, Pa," said Thad.

"I'll sit first watch," said Ballard. "And we can stuff some packs into Prine's bedroll to make it look like he's sleeping, then he can hide off in the woods somewhere nearby. Between the two of us we should be able to spot something. You fellers only pretend to sleep. You'll never wake up in time if something happens quick. I saw too many throats slit at Shiloh to think otherwise."

It was still too early to turn in, though the darkness of the woods made the hour seem later than it was. Prine and Ballard talked along the line Ballard had brought up: the Battle of Shiloh, where they had lost many companions and seen much death during the three-day conflict.

"Ballard, I recall a tree down close to the pond. The first part of the fight it was leafy and green. I saw the same tree after the battle. Not a leaf on it, and hardly a branch. And the pond was as red as blood where men had been washing their wounds. There were bodies all around. It's a sight I don't ever want to see again."

Ballard looked thoughtful in the growing darkness. "That's for sure, Prine."

Prine chewed on a twig. "You know, I hoped my killing days were over when the war ended. And they were, up to now. It's a painful thing, killing a man, even when there's no choice. I hope that nothing happens tonight. I saw enough death at Shiloh to last me the rest of my days."

"There's things that are worth killing for, Prine," said Stuart. "Don't you think a pile of money is worth a few dead outlaws?"

Prine studied the young man. "You're young, Stuart. Things seem different when you're young. Men were meant to live, not to die."

Stuart looked into Prine's face, then turned away without a word.

The night grew thick and black, though the moon managed to filter a little light between the trees. The men made out their bedrolls, cursing the lack of fire and light, and Stuart and Thad crawled in, adjusting themselves as Ballard had instructed. Prine thrust his saddlebags into his bedroll, moving them around until they approximated the shape of a sleeping man. Then he took his rifle and pistol into the woods nearby as Ballard sat down on an old stump, his shotgun across his knee.

Prine sat alone in the woods, staying out of sight but keeping an easy view of the camp. He could see Ballard's face through the leaves. His friend looked much older than when he had known him years before, his eyes weary and his skin weather-beaten. But still he was a strong man, perhaps even stronger than in his youth. He could hear the faint sound of the man singing.

> My own true love is gone away,
> Across the rolling water,
> And now I wander all alone,
> But I shall roam no farther,
> But I shall roam no farther.

The tune was soft and sad in the darkness, and made Prine feel old and tired. Suddenly he wasn't sure why he was there. Maybe it was because of Bob Stuart—yes, that was it. This was not for money, but for his old friend. It was a last tribute to his partner and a way of standing defiant in the face of time and death. Perhaps he wouldn't survive this quest, but even if he died it would be as he wanted it—fighting to the last, in a paradoxical way victorious in defeat.

His thoughts were interrupted by a rustling in the woods on the other side of the camp. Then there was silence, long enough to make him suspect that he had only imagined the disturbance. But it came again, at a slightly different location. Someone was there. Someone was moving about in the brush, trying to remain unseen. Ballard sat unmoving, as if he had heard nothing, but Prine knew better. His friend was as aware of the location of the noise as if he were looking at it. Prine saw Ballard's finger settle on the trigger of the shotgun.

Prine rose silently and began to move toward the other side of the camp, circling the clearing. He trod lightly, trying to make as little noise as possible. He wanted to surprise whoever was hidden across in the brush. His hand crept to the knife in his belt and unsheathed it. It felt good in his hand, sharp and well balanced.

His progress was slow. Ballard's back was still turned toward the hidden intruders, but when Prine had circled far enough to let him see the husky man's face, he saw alertness in his eyes. Stuart's face was also turned toward him, eyes open and muscles tense, though he kept the posture of a sleeper. Thad was no doubt as alert as the others.

Closer he crept, hoping he would give no sign of his presence. Perhaps he could get close enough to whoever it was to jump him, take him alive, and make him talk. Then the moonlight shimmered on the barrel of a revolver muzzle thrust out from the brush, pointed at Ballard's head.

That was it. Secrecy would be impossible if he wanted to save his friend's life.

Prine cried out a warning as he threw his knife hard at the spot just above where the barrel protruded from the leaves.

CHAPTER
7

There was great confusion immediately after Prine's throw. Ballard ducked quickly and rolled. The knife passed over him and thudded into something in the bushes. There was a groan and the sound of a falling body. Prine's blade had struck home.

Just as Thad and Stuart leapt from their bedrolls there was a scurrying, rushing sound in the woods, the noise of snapping branches and disturbed bushes. Someone was running away. Probably there were two of them, one either dead or wounded from Prine's blade, the other running for his life through the dark forest.

Ballard leapt up and ran along with Prine into the woods after the fleeing man. Prine mouthed quick instructions to Stuart and Thad.

"Head off and circle around right, toward the west. We'll try to head him off in that direction." The two young men obeyed, disappearing into the thicket.

Prine and Ballard gripped their rifles and ducked low branches, straining to see in the darkness. They couldn't let their prey escape; they needed to know how much information he possessed about their mission, and mostly if he were involved with or knew anything of the Tate gang. They had lost their previous chance for that type of information when Stuart killed the gunman in the ghost town.

There he was, heading around a thick clump of undergrowth. Ballard was quick as a running deer, an amazing achievement for a man of his size. Prine was growing hot, his brow covered with beads of sweat and his hair disheveled from brushing against unseen branches.

They lost sight of the man again. Perhaps he was hidden, trying to let them run past him. They stopped, panting and listening intently for some indication of where he might be. There was only the sound of their labored breathing and the night breeze in the treetops for a long while; then suddenly, several yards off to the left, they heard breaking branches and hurried, heavy footsteps. They took off in that direction.

He was heading up a wooden slope not far ahead. They could have dropped him with a shot, but that could have foiled their plan of taking him alive. And if by chance there were others in this forest, it might have drawn them.

Like a pounding buffalo Ballard dashed up the slope, Prine beside him. This must be a young fellow they were chasing; he seemed fleet and swift. But he was also scared, for he would never have been so loud in his escape had he been thinking clearly.

They crossed the crest and stopped again. Prine was out of breath, and his face and arms were bloody from many scrapes with brush and briars. He tasted sweat in his mouth, and his lungs ached as they sucked in the cool night air. But he couldn't stop now.

Farther off they heard him, running as swiftly as ever and heading west. Prine drew a deep breath and took off again, and Ballard thudded along beside him, his heavy strides shaking the ground.

They reached the spot where they had heard the fellow, but he was gone. On the ground Prine found a portion of the man's shirt, ripped from his sleeve by a protruding branch. He fingered it as he looked around, trying to guess which way the man had run.

It was more chance than anything else that led them off toward the southwest, dodging the smaller saplings that filled this portion of the woods. They ran for several minutes before Prine began to suspect that the man had not come this way. He stopped and conferred with Ballard.

"We'd best be careful—we might lose our way if we don't watch where we're going. I thought he came this way, but now I ain't too sure."

"Let's head due west. I think I heard something over there a minute ago."

Prine listened. Ballard was right—there was noise from the west. But from the sound of it, it wasn't a running man. Maybe he had slowed down, thinking that he had evaded them. Now would be the time to surprise him.

They headed in that direction, trying to keep their heads low and the noise down. It was hard to do; the leaves and twigs beneath their feet were invisible in the darkness, and at times they would step on some dry branch that would snap noisily beneath their weight. And now, fatigued as they were, it was hard to not gasp loudly for breath.

They moved down a few more yards, and then suddenly Ballard stopped. Prine didn't understand his friend's action, but he stopped beside him, tense and listening intently. Ballard's face showed sudden concern, as if he had heard something that disturbed him.

Prine heard it then, too. Men talking, and not in low voices. Then through the woods he saw the faint flicker of firelight. A group was camped about a hundred yards away, and from the appearance of things, was making only a token effort to remain unseen.

Ballard crouched. Prine did the same. "Who do you think . . . ?"

Ballard shook his head. The two men sat still, listening. They forgot the man they were chasing, for this discovery was a development they hadn't anticipated.

"Sounds like several of 'em—maybe five or six," Prine said. "It could be more. Do you think we should get closer?" Prine wasn't sure whether his friend would want to draw nearer and risk discovery. But Ballard nodded at the suggestion, and the two men rose, two dark and silent ghosts of the forest gliding toward the flickering light some distance away.

They were almost to the very edge of the camp when the thicket before them suddenly burst to life, moving suddenly and loudly. Prine hissed beneath his breath, startled like a man who unexpectedly hears a rattler at his feet.

But this was a human animal that made the noise, apparently the same one they had been pursuing, for he ran like a man in blind panic off to the left, leaving them too stunned to move or say a word.

"What was that? Somebody's out there!" The voices came from the camp, and there was sudden movement from that direction.

"Lord, this is a fine fix!" Ballard snorted low as he darted for cover. Prine jumped down beside him, and they hid behind a rotting log, thick bushes covering them on all sides. There was scarcely room enough for both of them, but there was no time to look for a better hiding place, for suddenly the woods began filling with armed men, searching the forest.

Ballard and Prine were on the very edge of the camp. Looking across the log they could see right into the clearing. Men were moving out of it with guns in their hands, scouring the forest in all directions. There was a blazing fire in the midst of the clearing, and the tantalizing smell of hot, boiling coffee reached them. But they took no notice of the aroma, for what they saw beside the fire caught their attention and confirmed the suspicion that had been growing in their minds.

A girl—a pretty young blond. And she held a gun and looked around at the dark forest. Prine could read her fear. Her hands twitched nervously on the butt of her pistol. She started occasionally when one of the searchers in the woods made some unexpected sound.

It could be no one else but Priscilla Tate. They had stumbled right into the camp of those they least wanted to meet.

Prine thought of Thad and Stuart, out there alone and unaware of the armed men who searched the forest. What if they should stumble right into their hands? It could be death for both of them.

Prine glanced over at his partner. Ballard was staring into the camp, watching the young girl—she seemed much younger and more delicate than Prine had anticipated—and the big man's expression was grim. His face showed fear, but Prine knew the fear was not for himself but for his son, who was out there somewhere and probably unaware of the danger.

Brush moved close beside them. A man was approaching, a pistol in his hand and his free arm knocking aside the brush as he searched. In only a moment he would be upon them.

CHAPTER

8

One bush stood between them and detection. Prine gripped his rifle; that fellow might find them, but he wouldn't live to announce his discovery to the others. Not that it really mattered—the shot would draw them anyway—but Prine would not go to his grave without taking someone with him, nor would Ballard.

He prepared to fire as he saw the hand come around the bush, gripping the branches to push them aside. But before that fateful move was made the unexpected roar of a shot, then another, came echoing through the forest from some distance away. The hand withdrew suddenly, and the man moved away at a run. Prine and Ballard were saved from discovery, at least for the moment.

But neither took time to ponder their good fortune, for they were filled with concern about those shots. At whom had they been aimed? Thad and Stuart? Prine hoped not, but it was hard to feel optimistic. Ballard must be in a horrible turmoil right now, Prine thought. His son was out there in the forest, perhaps wounded or dead.

They could hear voices coming loudly from the darkness behind them. The girl still crouched beside the fire, listening. Prine looked at her face. What he saw wasn't what he expected, based on what Stuart had said. She didn't look like the kind of girl to be riding with a band of killers, searching for stolen wealth. Prine had expected to see hardness and cruelty in her, but he could detect only fear. She reminded him of a frightened fawn. And she was very pretty.

The men were moving as a group toward the camp now, carrying something between them. They strode past Prine and Ballard into the circle of light around the campfire. On the ground they dumped their burden. A body. The dead face fell toward Prine and Ballard.

It wasn't Stuart or Thad. It could be no one else but the same man who had earlier tried to get the packet, the man they had chased only minutes before. He was stone-cold dead. There was a spot of deep crimson on his chest.

"There he is, ma'am. We found him trying to hide in a clump of cottonwoods. You needn't worry about him no more."

The girl said, "Did you have to kill him? I didn't want anything like this."

"What did you expect us to do, lady? Shake his hand? This fellow double-crossed you. You hired him, then he and Thaxton decided to get it all for themselves, just like Bryant and Allen. He deserved just what he got."

The girl covered her brow with a slender hand. "I'm just not accustomed to this. I didn't think it would come to murder."

"Murder, you say? No, ma'am—this was just and fair execution. I'd say if there are any murderers in the light of this fire it's our dear departed friend Orville Beecher here. We found no trace of Thaxton. Likely as not Beecher killed him so he wouldn't have to split the take. It would be like him to do that. That's murder, lady—not this." He turned away. The girl said nothing, but looked despairing.

Another man spoke. "Do you think there could be others out there? There was an awful lot of crashing around a minute ago."

"I don't know, Harvey. Maybe. But they'd be long gone by now."

Another of the men was laughing, apparently drunk. Prine looked closely at the group. Not until then did he notice the careful, exaggerated movements of men that have had too much to drink. Apparently they had been tipping the bottle for quite some time now, for many of them staggered slightly and others sat quietly in a kind of daze. The man who had laughed spoke out in a loud voice.

"Ol' Beecher here was a bad sort, I reckon, but even a

dog deserves a funeral—and a wake! Buster, get out your fiddle! We'll have the derndest wake that ever was—and then you'd all best settle back, for I aim to preach me a sermon!"

Hooting and laughter came in response. The one called Buster moved over to his pack and brought out a dirty flour sack. From it he produced a battered fiddle, and he plucked the strings, twisting his face in concentration as he turned the pegs and brought the instrument into some semblance of good tune. Then he tightened up a bow that had as many loose hairs as good ones, and drew a cake of rosin across the taut horsehair. He dragged the bow across the strings with a scratchy sound that quickly melted into the smooth, mellow tones of an old fiddle tune.

He began tapping his foot and sawing hard on the catgut strings. Not ones to worry about hiding themselves, this bunch! They were singing, some dancing, and the whiskey was flowing freely. And off to the side sat the young, pretty Priscilla Tate, apparently disturbed by it all, and looking out of place.

Prine realized how drunk these men were, and the amount of liquor they were consuming would only make them wilder. Several were dancing crazily, reeling around the fire, hooting and stomping out of rhythm with the fiddle, making so much noise that the music was hardly audible.

"This is for you, Beecher!" one of them shouted. "Show some life, boy! Get up and dance!" They laughed hard at that. Priscilla Tate buried her head in her hands.

"Why, boys, I don't believe old Beecher is aiming on dancing with me!" the fellow continued. "Somebody had best explain to him that that ain't nice! Harvey, give me a hand here. I'm going to teach ol' Beecher how to step to the music!"

Harvey quickly moved to the body and hefted it up. The head fell back, mouth open, as he dragged the gruesome corpse over to the dancing man and pushed it into his arms. He supported its weight and began moving about, holding the body around the waist. The feet dangled, swinging in a wild, loose parody of a dance. All the while the other men laughed and clapped, drinking from bottles, jugs, canteens, and anything else that would hold liquor.

"That's the way, Beecher! You sure know how to liven up a wake!"

"Step lively, now, Beecher!"

"Stomp them feet good, boy!"

The sight was appalling, but the men seemed not to notice or care. This was a rough, wild crew, and somehow Prine could feel only pity for the pretty young lady involved with them. It didn't seem natural for her to be there. She sat to the side, an image of dejection, as the wild celebration continued.

"Boys, I believe Beecher's getting tired of dancing!" the man shouted. He suddenly flung the body away from him, and the corpse fell limply and hard onto its back with a loud thud. One hand fell into the fire, but no one seemed to notice.

"That's right, Beecher. You rest a while. You've got a right to be tired after dancing like that!" The fiddle screeched on.

After the party had continued for some time, the man who had originally started the celebration walked forward, raising his arms above his head and looking at the rugged assembly with mock earnestness. The fiddle screeched out a particularly grating note and stopped. Orville Beecher's recent dancing partner quit his wild gyrations. The men gathered around the fire, and the mock preacher moved over to the body of Beecher and looked down on him for a moment.

"My friends," he began in a tremulous voice, "we are gathered here in the sight of God and man to lay to rest the body of the poor departed Orville Myron Beecher Jr., a man known and loved by each of us here." He paused, and from the crowd came a muttered "amen" and "God rest his poor soul."

The Preacher's hands moved to his chest and he stood with stomach protruding and thumbs hooked into his armpits. "A good, good friend he was, and a wonderful provider for his family, and he shall certainly be missed by all of us. But mostly he shall be missed by his two lovely babies and his lovely wife, wherever she is and whoever she is with tonight. But mostly, friends, all of us shall remember one thing about Orville Beecher: He was a truly marvelous dancer, a man with feet as light as sunrise and legs so muscled as to remind one of a buffalo . . ."

For long minutes the mock sermon continued. Prine lay there wondering how long this travesty would go on. Ballard nudged him and pointed over to the group of seated men. Two of them were asleep in a drunken stupor, and from the looks of the rest of them it would be a matter of only minutes before the same condition overtook the entire group. Even the Preacher was tottering a little more with each word.

". . . and so, friends, let our dear dead brother be a lesson to each of you . . . do not start on the horrid road of crime, for in the end it will kill you and destroy your soul . . ."

He was getting fired up now, his voice flowing like water over a mill wheel, spurred on with the enthusiasm of an old-fashioned pulpit-slapping preacher. All the while his congregation of ruffians were drifting off one man at a time into a deep, drunken sleep, their cries of "amen" and "you tell 'em, Preacher" growing ever fainter.

Priscilla Tate was on her side now, apparently dozing, though her hands were over her ears, as if to block out the sound of the funeral oration. The Preacher was winding to a close.

". . . and so now, friends, let us always remember our departed brother in love—good lands, Beecher, you've got your hand right in the fire . . . here, let me kick it out for you—and do what we can to ensure that his memory is always held dear to those who . . . who . . ."

From the sudden glazing of the speaker's eyes, it was clear what was coming. He swayed like a great oak in a storm, then stiffly fell, out before he hit the ground, landing directly atop the subject of his eulogy. He began to snore in deep, rich tones.

Prine and Ballard quietly slipped away from their hiding place and moved swiftly through the dark forest.

Behind them the campfire flickered fainter and quickly burned down to glowing red coals that cast a strange light on Orville Beecher, his unconscious mourners, and the lonely-looking lady with them.

CHAPTER
9

They found Thad and Stuart in a thicket about halfway back to the camp.

"I'm glad to see you!" exclaimed Thad. "We thought maybe they had shot you."

"It wasn't us they shot—it was that fellow we were chasing. We thought at first it was *you* they got. Stuart, that was the Tate gang. We saw Tate herself with them."

"That's what I figured. We saw them coming through the woods and hid out here. That's when we heard the shots. But why did they shoot that fellow if he was one of them?"

"Because he had cut out on his own," said Ballard. "That fellow Prine killed and this fellow were trying for the prize themselves. The others made short work of him when they found him."

"At least he had a funeral."

Ballard flashed a sardonic glance in response to Prine's comment.

"Well, if the Tates are that close, then we should get out of here fast," said Thad. "They could find us before morning."

"We don't need to worry about them tonight, Thad," said Prine. "They're drunk as sailors, passed out on the ground. All but the lady herself. And they have no idea we're this close by, I think. If they did they would sure have been more careful about their little party. The best thing we can do is get some rest."

They went back to their camp. In the brush beside the clearing they found the body of the man whose life had been cut short by Prine's blade. Prine retrieved his weapon, cleaned it, and then joined Thad in dragging the body into the clearing

He didn't recognize the face. The fellow had a mustache and hair touched with gray. Prine glanced at Stuart.

"They said his name was Thaxton. You know him?"

"Never saw him before. I'm not acquainted with any of the Tate bunch except by reputation."

Prine said, "Just how much do you really know about this Tate girl, Stuart? She didn't look the type that you described. I had the feeling that she wasn't used to being around men of that type at all. In fact, she looked downright miserable about the whole affair."

Stuart shook his head violently. "Don't let appearances deceive you, Prine. She's as hard as they come. Why would she assemble a bunch like she's got if she weren't? She's a devil, one that will give us a lot more trouble before this thing is over."

The young man turned away, apparently and surprisingly perturbed, as if any hint of defense of Priscilla Tate, no matter how tentative and hypothetical, made him angry. Prine was taken aback by the show of emotion, but said nothing as he began searching through the pockets of the dead man. Just what he sought he didn't know, but it made no difference, for the man carried nothing.

Ballard and Prine picked up the body, carried it off into the forest, and dumped it in a gully.

When they returned to camp, Thad was in his bedroll and Stuart sat on the stump at guard duty. "You get some rest," he told them. "Ballard, you can replace me in a couple of hours."

Ballard lay quietly, not far from Prine. His eyes were sad, and his head was cupped in his hands. He stared up silently through the branches as he lay on his back. Above, the stars flickered in the blackness of the sky, and occasionally across his vision flashed dark things, creatures of the night, moving silently across the heavens in search of other night creatures that would become their prey. Ballard closed his eyes and tried to sleep.

Prine was awake, too, his thoughts occupied by the girl name Priscilla Tate. She wouldn't leave his mind for a moment. When he had looked at her from his hiding place beside the camp, she had looked like a girl trapped in something that was now beyond her control, and he could not view her as an enemy, no matter how he tried. He felt a strange pity for the young lady.

"I must be getting soft and old." He whispered the observation to himself, then hoped no one had heard him.

He rolled over on his side and stretched his tired muscles. Sleep began to steal over him, and soon he was slumbering. He dreamed later that night, seeing Priscilla Tate standing over him, a gun in her hand, preparing to kill him. Then, just as her finger squeezed down on the trigger, she flung the weapon aside and disappeared, leaving him alone and mystified. It was a strange dream, and made Prine stir fitfully in his sleep.

Ballard still could not rest. He lay quietly, though, aware that even a sleepless man could arise refreshed if he avoided the temptation to tumble about all night. And besides, soon it would be time to replace Stuart at sentry duty, so sleep was somewhat pointless anyway.

Stuart. Now there was a man Ballard could not feel fully comfortable around, He was certainly a cocky and able fellow, yet mysterious too. Ballard's instincts had guided him accurately all of his life, but now they seemed to be failing him, for he could find no category in which to place the young man. He found no obvious reason not to trust him, but still he was cautious, afraid to rely on him without reservation.

"You should be more trusting," Ballard's wife had told him time and time again. Perhaps she had been right, he thought. Maybe he was overly suspicious by nature. But still, caution had saved him many times from disasters of all types, and trusting the wrong person could easily be a fatal move.

After several more minutes came the noise of movement from the other side of camp. Stuart had risen, his rifle in his hands. Ballard started to rise to see what had stirred the young sentry, but then he stopped. He twisted his head slightly so he could see Stuart's form in the darkness.

Stuart was looking over the reclining figures before him, as if trying to decide if they were truly asleep. For a long time he stood there. Ballard tried not to move. Stuart looked once more at each of the men, then turned and stared into the forest.

Lifting his rifle and holding it close to him, he stepped quietly toward the dark trees, as silent and sly as a cat. Now that was a strange move for sure, Ballard thought. He sat up carefully, now wide awake. Why would Stuart leave his post with such obvious stealth? And what could inspire him to head out into the woods alone at a time like this, leaving the camp unguarded?

Ballard sat listening. He heard the faint tramp of Stuart's feet on the forest floor, moving away toward the southwest. He was obviously not trying to be silent now that he was away from camp, at least not to the extent he had been before. Ballard was struck with a strong feeling of suspicion.

He rose from his bedroll and slipped on his boots, debating whether to wake Prine. He reached over to nudge the sleeping man, but suddenly he pulled his hand back, paused indecisively, picked up his shotgun and moved off alone.

He headed into the trees at the same spot he had seen Stuart enter. His eyes squinted in the darkness, and for a time he could see nothing. But to the southwest he thought he could make out a moving form in the darkness. He tried to remain silent as he headed toward it.

It was Stuart, all right. The young man gripped his rifle tightly, and from his crouched stance Ballard could tell he was again trying to move swiftly and silently. And what was more, he was traveling toward the Tate camp.

Ballard stayed behind in the shadows of the trees. There was only the noise of the night birds and the faint rustling of the wind.

What was that noise off to the left? Ballard heard it just as Stuart whirled around, and slid quietly behind a spruce as the young man searched the forest. Ballard stood like a statue, trying to breathe softly.

The noise came again, and Ballard saw a deer loping off through the night. Stuart saw it too, and relaxed. Stuart wheeled and began moving off in the same direction as before. After waiting long enough for Stuart to get some distance away, Ballard slipped from his hiding place and followed.

There could be no doubting one fact: Stuart was heading straight for the Tate camp. Why? Was he aiming to take on the whole gang at once? Then Ballard was struck with a sudden realization: The gang was asleep, and not with the normal, light sleep of men on the trail, but with a heavy, drunken stupor. And Stuart knew that, for they had told him. The horrible possibility of what Stuart just might be planning came to Ballard, and he was appalled. He remembered the way Stuart had cruelly shot one surrendering man. Killing didn't seem to bother the fellow. That put a bad taste in Ballard's mouth.

He couldn't let him do it. The men Stuart was seeking to kill were killers themselves, and heartless ones at that, but if Stuart were planning on shooting them in their sleep, he was no better than any of his prospective victims. Ballard wouldn't stand for it. He had to stop him. But how could he make his presence known without becoming the first victim of Stuart's gun?

That problem was suddenly eliminated, for a branch snapped loudly beneath Ballard's foot. Stuart whirled, his rifle up.

"Who's there?"

There was nothing to do but face up to him. "It's Ballard. Don't shoot!"

"Why did you follow me?"

Ballard's mind worked fast. "I thought I heard a noise, and I saw you get up to investigate. I thought you might need some help."

Stuart lowered his gun, but he looked angry. "Why didn't you make your presence known?"

"I didn't want to tip off anybody that might be in the woods. And besides, I wasn't sure it was you."

Stuart was cooling off, relaxing. Then he suddenly realized that he had some explaining to do.

"I heard a noise, too, and I thought some of those Tate gang members might have come up to camp. I would have woke you, but I wanted to be sure before I stirred everyone up." He approached Ballard as he talked. "I guess I was wrong. It must have been that deer back there poking around for food."

Ballard's instincts were sounding an alarm in his mind, but his voice remained calm. "Yep . . . I expect it was."

Without another word the pair headed back toward their camp.

Minutes later Ballard was seated on the stump with his shotgun across his lap, studying the sleeping Thomas Stuart, trying to piece together the strange puzzle of this man. Many of the pieces didn't fit, but a few were joining themselves together neatly. And the picture that came out made Ballard uncomfortable.

He resolved to keep a close eye on Stuart from that time forward. He would say nothing of what he had seen, at least not yet, for he could not be sure of the accuracy of his suspicions. But he would be watching, very closely.

Sunrise sneaks in like a slinking cat in Colorado, and this morning the sun's beams shone down on a group of sleeping men. Ballard sat slumped over on the stump, his gun still across his knees, his snores low-pitched. Prine stirred fitfully, and Thad and Stuart lay almost as still as one Orville Beecher only a short distance away. The morning was heralded by the music of birds.

Prine awoke abruptly, conscious of the sunlight on his face. It wasn't a feeling he was accustomed to when waking up, for usually he rose before dawn and was at his breakfast when the first rays peeped over the eastern horizon. But he had been bone-weary when he retired, and fatigue had overruled habit. From the looks of the other men the same had held true for them.

Prine rubbed his eyes and looked around. He grinned when he saw the hulking bear-like form of John Ballard dozing at his post. It could have been a dangerous thing, he realized, but last night there had been no real threat to their camp—only a bunch of outlaws who did not suspect their presence, and who were so drunk that they wouldn't have known Prine or Ballard from their grandmothers had they stood before them.

Prine grinned devilishly. He looked around and plucked a small, feather-like leaf from a wild shrub growing nearby. He crept toward the slumped-over Ballard, carefully slipped the leaf beneath his nose, and began tickling the sleeping man gently.

Ballard snorted in his sleep, his broad nose wrinkling.

He rubbed a huge, hairy hand against his face, then with a canine woof awoke, leaping up and knocking Prine aside unwittingly. His eyes were bloodshot and bleary, and for a moment he looked like a man who had been suddenly set down in the midst of an unknown country. Then he saw Prine.

Prine was grinning like a cat with a blue jay in its jaws; Ballard scowled back at him and swore. His voice stirred Thad and Stuart from their sleep, and they sat up bleary-eyed.

Breakfast was cold and the mood of the men was generally far from pleasant. Prine was the sole exception; for some reason he felt rather jovial this morning, though it was a joviality built on a foundation of caution and a very real sense of the danger that they might face later. His mind wandered to the group that had presented such a drunken spectacle the night before. This morning there would be no laughing and singing in that camp—only the nursing of headaches as big as the Rockies.

Ballard and Stuart were strangely quiet and sullen. Prine fancied that they avoided each other's glance. Lazily he pondered the mystery, but it seemed a minor affair. Probably they were both still tired from the exertion of the day before, and the threat of the Tate gang had doubtlessly worn on their nerves.

Ballard was grumbling again because of the lack of coffee. Prine had to admit that it was one luxury he too was missing right now, but there was no point in dwelling on it, for there was certainly nothing they could do about it. By nightfall they would be in Statler, and there perhaps they could have coffee. And if the coffee they brewed there were half as powerful as the town's reputation, then that would be one mighty strong brew.

"Just how close do you reckon the Tate bunch thinks we are?" asked Thad.

Prine swallowed a piece of jerky that tasted like shoe leather. "I can't be sure, Thad, but I don't think they realize how close we are. My guess is they're heading for Statler, hoping to find us there."

Ballard finished his breakfast and pulled a twist of tobacco from his pocket. He bit off a large chunk and settled it into his jaw. "I expect we'll have some trouble in Statler. That's a rough town."

"Well, why don't we avoid it, then?" Thad asked. "Just bypass it and go on."

Prine shook his head. "That's not what we need to do. Right now we got no gold on us, nothing but ourselves. If somebody is trying to give us trouble, now's the time to take care of them. The thing to avoid is letting them set the terms of the fight. In Statler we can set a trap and let them walk into it, instead of just waiting for them to jump us out in the mountains."

Thad looked concerned. "I was looking forward to Statler so I could get a hot bath and sleep in a read bed," he said. "Now I'm not so sure I want to go."

The men rode the rest of the day and did not encounter anyone. The country was wild and overgrown. The group fell into the same order it had followed during the preceding portions of the journey. Ballard was in the lead, and thus his face was invisible to the rest of them, but if any had been able to see it they would have noted an expression of worry. Ballard's thick brows were lowered, and his mouth tightly set in a line. He could all but feel the gaze of Stuart burning into the back of his head.

It was about Stuart that Ballard was thinking. Particularly he thought about the strange action of the young man the previous night. Clearly Stuart had been lying when he said he heard a sound in the woods, for Ballard had been awake and knew there had been no sound. And the careful scrutiny with which Stuart had studied his sleeping companions was not the response of an alert sentry to a sudden noise; it was the calculated and careful move of a man doing his best to avoid detection.

Ballard figured that Stuart knew of his suspicions. Something in Ballard wanted to tell Prine about all of this, but he stopped short of that. This was not the time . . . not yet.

The trail was narrow here, and every man in the party was on edge. They knew the danger of these wildlands. There was never a time that bandits did not haunt this region. Perhaps they would be ambushed up ahead, perhaps not.

As the sun westered in front of them, shining deep orange into their eyes, they saw Statler appear down the slope, the main street opening to engulf them like a hungry mouth. Prine thought about Priscilla Tate and her men. It was possible that they were still behind them on the trail, but again they might have avoided the road and cut through the forest itself—a more dangerous but much shorter route. If that were the case, then they might already be there in the hellhole before them.

Statler was a town just waking up with the sunset. Saloons lined the streets, more than Prine had ever seen in one town. This was the last of the West's lawless towns, a throwback to the Dodges and Tombstones of years past.

Many were the stares that the men drew as they plodded down the street, and greedy and hungry were the looks of many of the watchers. How much did this town know of what they carried? No doubt the local thieves considered any new arrival as a potential gilded chicken waiting to be plucked. Prine hoped they did not realize just how valuable were these chickens' feathers. Ballard carried a sawed-off shotgun across his saddle, daring any of the onlookers to move.

Prine looked hard into the faces of the men who stood about them on the boardwalk. He thought of Priscilla Tate again. She would be here, in the midst of this hell town. It didn't seem right. Not for a pretty young girl like her.

"Get hold of yourself, Jeremy Prine," he muttered beneath his breath, reminding himself that Priscilla Tate was probably a killer. It was definitely a group of killers with whom she associated. Her father had been a member of one of the West's most cruel and bloodthirsty gangs, and she herself sought to thwart a mission that was lawful and right. She didn't deserve pity.

But it didn't matter. Prine had seen the fear in her face last night in the camp, and he thought of her not as an outlaw but as a lady. And this was no place for a lady at all.

Before them was a hotel. It was a remarkably tall one for a town of this sort, three stories high and nicely painted. It looked out of place amidst the gaudy glow of the tawdry saloons and dance halls like a church in the middle of a circus. Prine tethered his horse in front of it and walked inside. Stuart went with him, while Ballard and Thad stayed outside with the horses. Ballard's sawed-off shotgun lay in the cradle of his crossed arms, looking deadly and threatening.

Prine and Stuart looked over the lobby of the hotel. It was fancy, almost elegant. The man behind the counter was dressed sharply, and his voice had an educated edge.

"Good evening, gentlemen. How many rooms?" He flashed an artificial smile that years of practice had rendered almost convincing.

"Two, please. Side by side." Prine glanced over at Stuart. "We need to stay close together."

"Fine, then. You'll have Rooms Five and Six, directly up the stairs facing the lobby. There is a connecting door between the two rooms."

Prine took the keys and looked upstairs. The doors to their rooms were visible from the lobby, opening right out onto the landing. The landing became a hallway off to the right, leading past one more door before making a right-angle turn toward the back of the building. Prine asked if anyone were in that third room, and was pleased to receive a negative reply. He didn't want anyone close beside them during the night.

"I like this setup," he told Stuart. "Better to be facing the lobby than to be hidden away back in a corner like a rat in a nest."

The pair turned and headed back toward the street. Halfway out the door Prine turned and called back to the clerk: "You got a stable here, or do I have to use the town livery?"

"There's a stable out back, sir. And the watchman is an alert man and a teetotaler." The clerk flashed his imitation smile again.

Prine and Stuart stepped out onto the boardwalk and rejoined Thad and Ballard. Music carried to them from a myriad of saloons, mixing into a dissonant conglomeration of sound.

CHAPTER

11

Ballard pulled the door shut behind him and locked it. He turned to look at the others standing in the hotel room. Stuart and Thad looked wary and apprehensive. Prine's features were unreadable. Ballard sat down heavily in a chair in the corner.

"Well, Prine, what now?" An unspoken assumption seemed to have arisen that Prine was the man who made the decisions, at least in Statler.

He sat down on the edge of the bed. "I didn't see anyone out there that I recognized as part of the Tate gang, but I'm sure they're here. Whether they'll come looking for us I'm not sure, but it don't matter—I plan to draw them to us."

Prine rubbed his chin. "They know only you by sight, Stuart. We could always use you as bait, but I don't want to risk that. Ballard and me are more used to this type of thing, I think. I believe I have a plan that should draw them like bugs to a candle."

The men gathered as Prine spoke in low tones. The plan he outlined sent a prickle of fear down the spine of everyone there, but each recognized the logic of it. At the end there was general assent on the idea.

Outside, the town of Statler grew wilder, and the noise of a gunshot echoed down the street. Few of the stragglers in the street noticed, and none of them cared.

Ezekiel Statler had first built his trading post and saloon in these parts in 1847, and from that time on the

54

place had grown. The men who came there were for the most part rowdy, strong characters, most just a shade on the wrong side of the law. But Ezekiel Statler had taken them in with no questions asked, and his trading post became the refuge for much of the scum of the West.

When the old man died the tradition continued just the same, and the town that sprang up bearing his name remained a haven for drunkards, bandits, horse thieves, cattle rustlers, prostitutes, and card sharks.

It was toward the end of the nineteenth century now, and law was commonplace across the West. But not at Statler.

It had a sheriff, all right, just as legal as any other town. The only trouble was that the sheriff was also the town drunk, and his election had been pulled off as a joke. Many thought he didn't yet realize that he held office. He would sit in the back of the Black Ace saloon for hours, his head on the table and his hand wrapped around a near-empty whiskey bottle, and his badge shining from his tattered shirt. Occasionally it would fall off, but someone would, without fail, replace it.

Statler couldn't last. Everyone in the town knew that. It was the last of a dying breed of town. Already many of the wild cattle and mining towns were gone. Someday that would be true of Statler, but until that time the people there would continue to carouse drunkenly and toast the days that would never come again.

Four men sat in the Black Ace saloon, their faces hard and unsmiling. They had been on the trail for days, looking for the men who rode with Thomas Stuart.

They knew of the packet Stuart carried. They had followed his movements closely, and they were certain that he was here in Statler with his companions. But could they find them here? That was the one thing that worried them.

Except for the one named Buster. He was too worried about whether or not his fiddle was being stolen to think of anything else. He had left the instrument in the town livery, and from that time on he had worried about it. His laments were becoming an irritation to the rest of his friends, mostly because he refused to leave his liquor long enough to do anything about the problem.

The piano music was loud, and the flow of conversation and shouting made a steady hum in the place, occasionally rising to a roar. The men sat silently, except for Buster, watching the action all around them, and occasionally they would glance toward the door.

About ten o'clock two men walked through that door. Staggered, actually. One of them was a tall, powerful-looking fellow with dark hair and sideburns touched with gray. He was slender, but had enough heft about him to indicate that he was no weakling. But he was dwarfed, almost, by the fellow beside him, a huge, burly bear of a man with a graying beard and broad face. Both men were middle-aged and appeared roaring drunk.

They were almost comical, holding on to one another as they moved into the saloon, the big one singing and the other waving to the crowd as if this were a party held in their honor. The big one was loud, his voice carrying over the noise of the other saloon occupants.

"Prine, my friend, let me buy you a drink! Then you can buy me one!"

The pair headed over to the bar, and the big man banged the polished bar top with such force that it rattled every glass on it and some on the nearby tables. It got the attention of the barkeep, all right, along with that of everyone else in the building.

"Whiskey! Good strong whiskey! The kind that pickles your guts and burns out your hair from the inside! That's what I want! And a whole bottle!" the big one demanded.

He got it. The husky fellow paid off and headed back across the saloon with his partner. They found a table in the corner, not far from the Tate gang members. Then they started in on the bottle of whiskey.

The big man talked on a myriad of topics, and all the while his partner did his best to keep him quiet. He would frown at him like a mother at a child, whispering "Hush" and "Keep your voice down!" and finally "Stuart will blow your head off if you talk too much!"

At that the four men sat up quickly. The name "Stuart" had gotten their attention.

"Nonsense, Prine!" bellowed Ballard. "I'm not worried about that runt's opinions. I'll do as I please, and Stuart be hanged! And why do you keep on telling me to hush? There ain't nobody in here listening to us . . . see, I'll show you."

The big man raised himself up and looked around without discretion, eyeing very closely everyone around him. He appeared so drunk as to be comical. But the four men at the nearby table were not laughing, though they listened and watched intently.

"See, Prine . . . nobody heard me." He pointed at a man near him. "Did you hear me? Or you? See . . . I told you they didn't hear me!" He glanced around toward Buster and his group. His face twisted into an exaggerated smile, and he reached up to tip a hat that wasn't there. "Evening, friends!"

They looked back with cold eyes, but he didn't seem to notice. He filled his shot glass to the brim again and drained most of it at a swallow. He sang for a while along with the piano, then began a drunken oration.

"Prine, we're going to be rich! Rich beyond our wildest dreams! And it's all out there just waiting to be picked up."

The four men at the nearby table glanced at each other, and smiles flickered across their faces. They listened closely to the blabbering big man and the other fellow who was so unsuccessfully trying to keep him quiet.

For a long time the show went on, the big one talking loudly and the smaller one trying to quiet him. Most of the men in the saloon paid no attention to them; most had not heard the big one's talk about wealth. But even the half-drunk Buster was paying close attention, though he tried to mask it.

One thing he didn't notice, though, was that after a full hour the bottle the pair were sharing was almost as full as when they began. His friends paid no heed to that strange phenomenon, either, not noticing that the sips taken by their drunken neighbors were quite small ones. Also unnoticed were the eyes of both men, eyes remarkably clear for men as drunken as these apparently were.

Abruptly the pair stood, walking away and taking their bottle with them. They moved out of the door of the saloon and on into the night. The four outlaws could hear their loud singing as they moved down the street. Then the immediate noise of the saloon drowned out the raucous music.

The four rose, wordlessly, and followed the pair out onto the street. On the boardwalk they looked in the direction the two had taken. They saw them only an instant before they disappeared into the next saloon.

"The fat one had a lot of mighty interesting things to say, now, didn't he!" grinned one of them. "It looks like they're making every saloon in town. And judging from the direction they're moving, I'd say they started from back this way—which means that they probably came from that hotel over yonder. Friends, I'd say that that hotel is where we'll find our friend Stuart—along with that map."

"Should we go after the two drunk ones, too?"

"Them two won't give us no trouble. And we should be able to handle the rest ourselves. Let's go."

They walked toward the hotel on the other end of town. None of them noticed the two men who stepped out of the saloon down the street, both cold sober. The pair moved like shadows after the four gunmen.

The whole scene was watched by Thomas Stuart from the alley window of Room 5. The building beside him cut off part of his view of the street, but when the four were almost in front of the hotel he saw them. And he also saw Ballard and Prine lurking behind them.

He dropped the curtain and moved quickly through the door that joined Room 5 with the next one. Thad was in there, busily at work on the thing they had been preparing since the two older men had left to act on Prine's plan.

"They're coming. Are you ready?"

Thad quickly finished his work. "I am now. Let's go."

The two young men headed back into Room 5 and picked up a chair. They sat it outside on the landing, facing the lobby, directly between the landing doors of Rooms 5 and 6. Thad sat down in it, his father's shotgun across his lap, his eyes fixed on the front door of the hotel. Stuart gave him a quick pat on the shoulder, then hefted his own rifle and stepped back inside one of the rooms, closing the door until it was only open a crack.

And then they waited.

The hotel clerk was locked away in the back office counting his day's receipts, so he did not notice when four men entered the lobby with their pistols drawn. Had he seen them he would have done nothing to stop them, for he had been in this town far too long and knew too well the type of men they were. He was not a strong man, nor a brave one, and that was why he was still alive in Statler. He had always hidden away from danger like a mouse in a corner.

So the lobby was empty when the gunmen came in, crouched and scanning the interior of the hotel. It took only a moment for them to notice the young man who sprang from his chair on the landing with a shotgun in his hands. And it took only a fraction of another moment for them to react with gunfire.

The bullets smacked close above Thad's head as he ducked into Room 6.

In the hotel's back office the clerk crawled under his heavy mahogany desk.

The four men scattered. One leapt behind the counter running parallel to the right wall and another hid against the opposite wall beside a heavy cabinet filled with fancy china and glassware. The remaining two headed immediately to the stairs and began running up toward the door Thad had entered.

They were halfway up the stairs when the short muzzle of a double-barreled shotgun poked out of the doorway and let go with a double roar. Two charges of shot ripped into the wall just above the heads of the two men, and they ducked, one of them losing his footing and tumbling down the stairs to roll out on the floor. But he was up in an instant, and he and his partner darted up the stairs and hugged the facing wall on either side of the Room 5 door. At a signal, both men leapt in front of the door and kicked it in.

A figure stood in the middle of the room, holding a rifle aimed directly at them. They opened fire immediately and riddled the tall form through and through with .44 bullets.

As the figure fell stiffly backward onto the floor, the men saw it for what it was: a dummy constructed on the back of a chair, set up in the middle of the room with a rifle in its lifeless arms. They had been fooled.

But another figure, this one very alive, bolted through the doorway in the back of the room that connected the room with the adjoining Room 5. In his hands was a sawed-off shotgun, reloaded and cocked. As he entered, the closet door on the other side of the room burst open and revealed another man hidden there, his rifle aimed at gut level toward the men.

The second of the Tate gunmen wanted to give up immediately, but was knocked aside by his partner, who made a desperate scramble for the doorway. He tripped and fell, and the other let panic override his urge to surrender and leapt across the fallen man onto the landing just outside the door. The downed man then leapt up and fired a shot that zipped close by Thad's head. In answer, a blast from the shotgun exploded, in unison with one from Stuart's rifle from the closet.

One man was caught full in the chest, the force of the shots kicking him up from the floor and sending him reeling backward onto the landing. He hit on his heels and staggered, the small of his back striking the landing railing. He fell over it backward, arms spread wide, flipped in the air, and landed facedown on the floor below with a loud crash. He moved once, then no more.

Thad bolted to the door, thrust the shotgun out, and sent the remaining charge hurtling down toward the man hidden behind the counter in the lobby below. The man ducked, and the wall behind him shredded with lead pellets, just as two quick shots from the man who had just escaped the room sent Thad back under cover again. By now one gunman was hidden just around the corner down the hallway to Thad's left, and his position effectively sealed Thad in his room.

One of the gunmen hidden downstairs darted suddenly toward the storeroom beneath the landing and directly below Room 6. Thad saw it, but was unable to get off a shot at the man.

In the storeroom the man listened to the sound of footsteps above him, and aiming at the spot where their sound came from, sent two slugs ripping through the floor of the room above. He heard a startled and angry cry from above, and the sound of feet pounding away from where the shots had entered. He followed the sound and sent another blast angling off in that direction.

Suddenly he found his own strategy turned against him, for rifle slugs came ripping down through the ceiling of the storeroom to splatter into the floor all around him. One grazed the side of his head, almost costing him an earlobe, and he turned to dart out into the lobby again.

He caught himself short about halfway out the door, though, for he saw them suddenly: the same pair that had been in the saloon, bursting through the hotel's front door.

He ducked back inside the storeroom and heard his partner behind the counter open fire. He joined the effort, firing around the edge of the door, and the two intruders were forced back into the night.

He expected at any moment to receive more fire through the ceiling above, but it never came. And in a moment he understood why, for he heard running feet on the landing above, and the blast of a shotgun, aimed, he guessed, at his partner hidden around the corner in the upstairs hallway. The pair in the rooms above were apparently trying to drive the man out of his hiding place, but the plan didn't work, for there was a return burst of fire, and suddenly the rooms above were occupied again.

The dark window of the storeroom shattered, and a big man came rolling across the floor toward him. The outlaw turned to fire at the man, but the shot missed by several feet, even though he was almost at point-blank range. He didn't wait for the rapidly rising bear of a man to completely gain his feet. He darted quickly across the lobby, bullets smacking around his heels, and threw himself over the hotel counter to join his partner hidden there. Bullets punctured the smooth and polished countertop, and he hugged the floor in fear.

Ballard stuck his head and arm around the side of the storeroom door and fired toward the counter and the man raising a gun from behind it. The bullet scarcely missed the man, but the gunman managed to squeeze off two quick shots at Stuart, who fired from the doorway of Room 5.

Ballard pulled his head back into the storeroom. He looked about the dark room. His eyes rested on a half-full kerosene lamp, and he was struck with a sudden inspiration. He grabbed the lamp, removed the chimney, and dug in his pocket for a match while cranking the wick out several inches.

Upstairs, Thad was reloading. He could do little to stop the man who fired at him from the corner of the hallway, for every time he tried to squeeze off a shot at him he was caught in the fire of the men behind the counter. And conversely, whenever he fired at them, the man around the corner blasted away at him at close range. Stuart was in the same predicament the next door down.

Where was Prine? Thad had seen no sign of him since he burst through the door alongside Ballard a few minutes before. Somebody was downstairs, firing on the outlaws from the storeroom. Perhaps it was Prine, or maybe Ballard. He suspected the latter, for the crack of the pistol sounded like that of his father's Colt.

What then of Prine? Had he deserted them? It didn't seem like something he would do, judging from what Thad had come to know of the man so far. Maybe he had some sort of plan. Maybe he would show up unexpectedly. If so, Thad hoped he would hurry, for as it was now it was pretty much a standoff.

From below came a sudden flurry of gunfire from behind the counter. However, it was not aimed at Thad and Stuart, but across at whoever was hidden in the storeroom. There flashed across the lobby something flaming and glowing that Thad could not identify. A shot sounded below the landing, and the burning thing shattered in midair,

sending a shower of flaming kerosene all over the counter
and the area behind it.

With a horrible howl one of the men leapt from behind
the counter, his left arm coated in flaming liquid, his right
hand desperately pounding the flames. All about him on
the floor was flaming kerosene. His partner remained
invisible, apparently huddling away from the flames, making no attempt to help his endangered companion.

Thad was in a clear position to fire at the man, but he
could not, for he felt pity for the unfortunate fellow. The
man had dropped his gun and was exposing himself as a
clear target because his pain made him forget the danger of
such a move. Thad would not shoot a man who couldn't
fight back.

The man ripped off the flaming shirt, casting it aside
and saving himself from any serious burns. But he could not
save himself from the slug that whistled through the lobby
from Stuart's gun, killing him before he hit the floor.

Thad glowered. It had happened again. Stuart had
again killed a man with no good chance to fight back.

The fight remained in full swing, and it would not stop
until more men were dead or wounded. Thad knew it and
accepted it. He thrust his shotgun around the corner of the
door and fired off a blast in the general direction of the man
hidden down the hall and around the corner.

The flames below had burned themselves out now, and
the remaining gunman behind the counter began firing
again. The death of the other man had changed little. It was
still a standoff.

Below, Ballard was disgusted that his kerosene lamp
ploy had been unsuccessful. He had wanted to force the
men to surrender, but his plan had been foiled. He knew it
was Stuart who had killed the man, for he had heard the
crack of a Winchester when the shot was fired, and Thad
was fighting with a shotgun. Rapidly Ballard's doubts and
suspicions about Stuart were growing into certainties.

Ballard thrust his head around the door and fired a fast
and ineffective shot at one of the two remaining gunmen.
He heard Thad's shotgun blasting upstairs and the noise of
shot ripping into the countertop.

Suddenly there was no more shooting. The silence was

almost painful in contrast to the bedlam of the past few minutes. Ballard could hear the pounding of his own pulse in his temples. He took advantage of the stillness.

"You out there! We'll give you this one chance to surrender! The same goes for you upstairs! There's no point in anyone else getting killed! Give up and we'll let you go."

The only answer was a quick shot from behind the counter. Ballard felt the sting of wood chips against his face, scattered by the impact of the shot striking the door frame. He ducked back inside.

"All right. You just set the terms!" Ballard fired off a shot around the doorway.

There was a tremendous scuffling upstairs—shouting, gunfire, general confusion. And the gunman behind the counter suddenly ducked, cowering in his hiding place.

Then, landing directly in front of the doorway to the storage room, a body fell from upstairs. Ballard knew immediately the man was dead. It was the gunman who had imperiled Thad and Stuart from around the corner of the hallway.

Upstairs, Prine holstered his gun. He had entered through the back of the building, climbing in the second-story hallway window from the roof of the woodshed built between the hotel stable and the building itself. He had surprised the gunman from the rear, and when the fellow responded in gunfire, Prine's shots had driven him from his hiding place to fall over the railing and land beside his partner, who already lay dead on the floor.

"Don't shoot! Don't shoot! I surrender!" The voice came from behind the counter. Ballard saw a pistol fly over the countertop to clatter onto the floor. He recognized the voice of the man who had played the fiddle at Orville Beecher's funeral—the one they had called Buster. Quickly he moved out of the storeroom and into the lobby.

Buster stood behind the counter, arms high in the air. Ballard took the man prisoner at gunpoint, glancing upward toward the landing to make sure that Stuart did not kill this one too.

Thad stood directly in front of Stuart's door, blocking his view of the lobby. Ballard knew the move was deliberate, and he flashed a grin at his son. Stuart glared at Thad from the doorway right behind him, fingering his gun in frustration.

They had a prisoner at last, a man who could tell them more about this gang of killers that stalked them. Maybe now a few questions could be cleared up.

Ballard led the prisoner upstairs and into Room 5. Below, in the office, the hotel clerk still cowered beneath his desk.

Buster's attitude changed rapidly from one of fear to a contemptuous, snarling defiance of the men who had captured him. That didn't bother Prine; all he wanted was information, and he intended to do anything short of torture to get it. He stood before the seated outlaw, looking tall and fierce, and his eyes said clearly that he expected no nonsense. Behind him on the bed sat Thad and his father, and Stuart stood behind them in the corner, his arms folded across his chest and a look of dissatisfaction on his face.

Prine gazed silently at the prisoner for a long time. "Well, Buster, your scheme didn't work out, did it?" The outlaw started noticeably when Prine spoke his name, and he said, "How do you know who I am?"

"Oh, Buster, we know a lot of things about you, things you would be surprised at. We know how many men you run with, who leads you, and what you're trying to do. And it looks like we've knocked a good-sized hole in your group." He grinned sarcastically. "You should be grateful to us, Buster. We could have killed you out there, but instead we were nice enough to ask you up for this little visit. Now you can repay our kindness with a little information."

"I'll say nothing," Buster said.

Prine slapped the man across his stubbly cheek, hard. The slap resounded in the room and Buster cried out sharply. Prine looked into the man's red-rimmed eyes. "This is no game, Buster. You're lucky to be alive. Now, you can talk decent or we can flail you within an inch of your life. It's your choice." Prine punctuated the end of his sentence with another ringing slap that knocked the slumping outlaw back upright in his seat again.

"Now, friend, you can tell us the one thing we need to know—just exactly what your group has in mind. I want details, specifics about the whole thing. And no nonsense. None at all."

Buster flashed his version of a defiant leer into Prine's face. His voice sounded like that of a snake. "You just got three of us, mister, and there's more left. And before you leave Statler you're going to die, every one of you, from your fat friend over there to that rattler standing over yonder." His gaze fell on Stuart, who stood tense and angry, a killing glitter in his eyes. The outlaw's face became ugly with hate.

"What's the matter, bush baby?" Buster laughed. "Take a look at your friend over there, men. You know what he is?" Every eye turned to Stuart in instinctive reaction to the outlaw's words. "I'll tell you, he's nothing more than a bastard and a son of —"

Prine had seen fast draws in his days on the range, but never had he witnessed anything like what occurred at that moment. Stuart's hand disappeared, blurring into invisibility with sheer speed, as it whipped to the gunbelt at his waist and drew out the Remington. Three shots exploded in the small room, filling the air with smoke and the acrid smell of burnt gunpowder. As the reverberations of the shots faded into silence Prine's gaze fell on the dead body of Buster, blown against the wall by the shots, the animal snarl still on his lifeless face. For a long, tense moment there was no sound but the faint hissing of Buster's last breath escaping his dead lips.

"You murdered him . . . shot him like a dog! You . . ." Ballard's voice failed him, and his rage found its outlet in the only way possible: He swung his huge arm and pounded his fist into Stuart's jaw.

The young man fell back on the floor, his gun still clutched in his hand. He came up quickly, cocking back the revolver's hammer. His face was red with rage as he aimed the gun squarely at Ballard's face.

Every man in the room froze. Ballard stared unflinching into the black eye of the threatening gun. Stuart trembled, almost tearful in fury; then slowly the gun lowered and he slipped it into his gun belt. He strode to the bed and sat down on the mattress, his head dropping to his hands. Ballard looked at him coldly and said nothing.

Prine tried to break the tension in the air with soft words. "Why did you do it, Stuart?"

The young man looked up at the others. His expression was different now.

"Isn't it obvious why I killed him? Prine, didn't you see him moving toward you?"

Prine was incredulous. "Are you loco? He was sitting in this chair the whole time. He wasn't moving at me."

"I didn't see him move either, Stuart," Thad cut in. "All I saw was you killing a man because he insulted you. It was murder."

Stuart snorted in contempt. "Murder! If I hadn't done what I did you would have seen murder. He would have snapped Prine's neck in a second. But I realize why none of you saw him moving at Prine—when he started speaking of me you turned and looked in my direction, every one of you. I was the only one facing Buster, and so of course I was the only one who saw him move."

Prine realized that Stuart was right. When the outlaw had begun his tirade against the young man, all of them had turned to face Stuart. It had been a natural thing to do, and it had given Stuart an alibi that could not be refuted. Prine knew that the young man was lying, but he could not prove it. Clever, this fellow.

"I don't care what happened—from this moment on Thad and me are out of this deal," Ballard said. "C'mon, Thad. Let's head for the stable and get our horses."

Prine looked long at Stuart. "I'm afraid I'll have to join them," he said. "This isn't the sort of thing I bargained for."

Ballard was already out on the landing when Stuart gave a contemptuous laugh. "I guess I was a fool to listen to my father. I took him seriously when he said that Jeremy Prine and John Ballard were men of honor. Let me remind you, men, that I told you this would be a violent affair from the outset. You were warned, but still you agreed to stick this out to the end. I can see now that my trust in your good faith was misplaced. I understand now that you are out to look after yourself, no matter what you promised me. Go ahead—leave. My father trusted you, and wanted you in on this, and every step you take away from here is like trodding on his memory. I thought more highly of you than this, but I was wrong."

Prine was cut deeply by the words. It was true . . . they had each given their word of honor to stick this thing out. He recalled his thoughts while he had sat at watch in the night—thoughts of how he was doing this whole thing for Bob Stuart. To back out now would be an insult to the memory of his friend.

"You're one to talk about honor!" Thad burst out. "How much honor has a murderer?"

Stuart looked at him coldly. "I told you he was moving at Prine. I did what I thought necessary to protect Prine's life. If you think me a murderer, then prove it."

Thad was silent, and Stuart continued. "It really doesn't matter what you think of me, gentlemen. A man's word of honor is binding, no matter what the circumstances. And if you're so concerned about murder, then ask yourself what it is if you leave me here without protection. The Tate gang will have me dead before morning, all because you backed out on your promise and left me to die. That would be murder, gentlemen. Can you live with that?"

When Stuart finished he knew he had them. He had cut them at their most vulnerable spot. He was not surprised when slowly the men moved back into the room.

Ballard was the first to speak. "All right, Stuart, you've made your point. I'll see you through, just as I promised. But let me make it clear that I fully believe what you did was murder, and if you die before this business is finished it will be no more than what you deserve."

Stuart eyed him with anger. "In days not too long past those would have been fighting words, Ballard," he said. "Maybe when this affair is through we'll revive those days for a while."

"Nothing could please me more, Stuart," the hefty man said. He looked over at his son. "Thad, don't feel that you have to stay on if you don't want. I'll not force my son to help on a murderer's quest."

"I gave my word, too, Pa. I'll stay."

Prine said, "And I'll stay, too, Stuart. You make me sick to my stomach, but for the memory of your father I'll stay on."

"And I'm sure my father would be pleased," Stuart said. He swept his gaze across the group. "My popularity is totally unimportant here," he said. "But I do need your help, and I'm glad you're staying with me."

He stood and stretched. "We're all tense and angry right now. I'll carry out the body of our friend, and then I suggest we all get some rest. This whole thing won't seem so terrible in the morning."

Prine stood and moved toward the dead body in the corner. "Never mind, Stuart. I'll take care of it. I could use some fresh air before I turn in."

He picked up the dead body. He hefted the corpse over his shoulder and stepped out onto the landing and on down the stairs.

The town's undertaker already was below, and beside him the pale and shaken hotel clerk. The three bodies of Buster's partners were laid out in a row across the floor, and Prine walked over and dumped his burden beside them.

"Here's another one for you, mister," he told the undertaker. The man smiled and tipped his hat in thanks.

He stepped over to the front door and out into the street, breathing the cool night air. He was mildly surprised that the gun battle had not drawn much of a crowd, but in Statler shootings were normal fare.

He stood on the boardwalk and pondered the situation he and his friends found themselves in. He had hoped that the gunfight would end the threat of the Tate gang once and for all, but now things seemed as bad as ever. There were still three of the gang living, besides Tate herself. The Tate gang wasn't gone, only temporarily weakened. They would make no move tonight, he guessed, but tomorrow would bring Prine and his partners to Jericho Mountain. Surely the Tate gang would be there too, perhaps more determined than ever to get their prize.

"Why did you get me into this, Bob?" Prine asked the night. No answer came back.

It was then he noticed her, on the edge of the crowd milling about before the saloon down the street. From the appearance of things a cockfight had drawn the crowd, for men cheered and cursed alternately in a circle in the street. The blond girl, however, was looking not at the commotion but at Prine, and when he returned her gaze he saw fear in her eyes. She turned and moved into the throng.

It was Priscilla Tate. Prine moved quickly, darting toward her. He elbowed his way through the mass of yelling, hooting men, and he saw her moving before him, her blond hair bobbing along as she ran out of the other side of the crowd.

Prine forced his way through the throng and fell into pursuit.

CHAPTER
14

Prine was slowed by the stragglers and drunks who roamed the Statler streets. He darted through them like a man dodging trees in a forest, but the girl running ahead of him steadily increased her lead. She ran swiftly and cast frequent glances over her shoulder at her pursuer.

Statler's main street was long and well lit from the numerous saloons, faro parlors, and dance halls that lined it, so it was not hard for Prine to follow the girl. His breath came hard as he ran, and beads of sweat broke out on him. As the girl neared the end of the street, she turned suddenly and darted into a dark building, apparently some sort of deserted structure. There was no front door or shutters, and the unpainted building looked dismal in the darkness.

Prine headed after her. Why was she running? She didn't know who he was, though probably she had guessed he was part of Stuart's group. He realized that none of the Tate gang really knew any of his own party except Stuart himself. The shoot-out in the hotel had been the first face-to-face encounter between the rival groups. So Priscilla Tate was running from a man she didn't know.

Prine headed down the street at a trot and entered the dark building. He could see nothing at all because of the blackness of the interior. He stopped within a few feet of the door and stood in the midst of the dark room, listening closely for any noise that might betray the girl's hiding place. There was no sound but the faint scurrying of a rat off in some corner. But he knew she was here.

For a long time he stood still as a statue. He then

realized that he was probably silhouetted against the dim light of the street behind him. She was watching him against that background; he could almost feel her gaze. He edged silently to the right and into the thicker blackness of the shaded wall beside him. Still there was no hint of life within the building. Prine wished he could see catlike into the blackness and find her.

A chilling thought came. What if she was armed? The more he thought about it the more certain he became that she was. This was Statler, and few people, women included, dared venture into the streets without some means of protection.

Then there was a sudden flurry of movement from the opposite corner of the dark room. He moved forward. Two rapid shots blasted into the stillness of the room: cracking shots, fired from a derringer.

Prine felt the bullets whistling by him in the darkness, and drew in his breath sharply. He ran toward the spot from which the two flashing bursts of gunfire had exploded seconds before, and his hands brushed the softness of long, feminine hair and the slender shoulder of a girl. But she was quick and nimble, and turned out of his grasp. He fell against the rough wall.

She was gone. He saw her faint form as his eyes grew more accustomed to the darkness. She ran toward the back of the building, then a door opened, revealing her for a second against the shining night sky. The door closed and Prine was alone.

He moved toward the door, bumping his shin against something and falling to his face on the floor. The place was covered with filth and trash, and Prine landed facedown in the midst of it. He stood quickly, brushed the mess off of him, and continued the chase.

His hands groped the wall, searching for the latch that marked the door. There . . . he found it. Quickly it gave under his strong hand, and the door opened into the night. He exited swiftly.

Where could she be? Her escape had given her a good lead and a strong advantage. She might well have already disappeared into the throngs in one of the saloons. But he could look for her. It would be worthwhile to have a talk with the girl whose men had done their best to kill him and his friends earlier tonight.

He was in the back streets of Statler now, and the buildings looked remarkably different from their false fronts that faced the main street. They appeared rough and crude when viewed from this angle—shabby buildings. Trash was strewn throughout the overgrown rear areas of the buildings, and Prine winced at the foul odor of the mess. He saw the flashing eyes of a cat as it roamed the area, searching for the rodents that thrived in the trash heaps.

Prine moved into an alley that led back to the main street. He heard a low groan at his feet, and started in surprise, as if he had nearly stepped on a rattler. He looked down and saw a man reclining there, drunk as a sailor, his hand around a half-empty bottle. Prine felt disgust mixed with pity. No doubt this fellow lay drunk in some alley every night. But such was life in Statler.

He walked quickly back onto the main street. There was no sign of a blond head among the crowds, and Prine was fearful that the girl had escaped him. He turned to glance in the opposite direction.

He saw a sudden flash of yellow at a corner. He ran toward it, mildly surprised that the figure did not try to run. He grasped the shoulder and wheeled the person around, then stared into the face of a grimy, bearded man who had apparently not had a shave or haircut in months. He looked dull and dissipated. He appeared old, yet the thick blond hair told Prine that this was a young man, aged only by liquor and the opium available in Statler's back-street dives. The man's eyes registered not a trace of surprise at Prine's unexpected jostling.

"Sorry," Prine muttered. He turned away.

She was gone. Vanished into the crowd. He stopped the pursuit and leaned against a post to catch his breath. He looked, bewildered, at the many saloons that lined the street. If she were in one of them it might take all night to find the right one. And he had no proof that she was in any of them.

This had been a wild night, and he was only beginning to realize how tired he was. There had been little real rest for the group since this adventure had started just short of three days before. Three days! Yet it could have been a month. Prine was growing very weary.

He walked slowly down the street. He glanced up randomly, and took in the side of a stable back some distance off the street. There was a large window in the side, crisscrossed with rusted metal bars. Through that window he could see the lantern-lit interior of the building, and there he saw her. She was talking rapidly to someone. She seemed disturbed.

This must be the place she and her gang are holed up, he thought. He stopped in his tracks, debating what to do. Should he go back to the hotel and get the others? No . . . especially not after Stuart's demonstrated penchant for murder. Somehow Prine couldn't let him have a chance at Priscilla Tate. Prine felt that vague and unexplainable tenderness toward her that he had first felt in the forest, hidden with Ballard beside her camp. He would check this out himself. Besides, there was no point in risking the life of all of them, he rationalized.

He looked for entrance to the stable. There was a front door, but it was closed, and walking through it would be an invitation to quick death, anyway. Perhaps there was a back way. He crept to the side of the building, crouched under the window, and glanced cautiously inside.

She was seated on a crate inside. Three men were with her, and Prine recognized them from the forest camp. One of them was the man who had preached Orville Beecher's unorthodox funeral. The other two he could not attach a name or label to, but their faces were familiar.

Prine looked toward the back of the stable. There was a large rear door, open to the night, and beyond a field overgrown with weeds. A wagon sat halfway inside the doorway, its rear portion outside. Prine quickly formulated a plan.

He trotted quietly around the side of the building toward the rear. He rounded the corner and came up beside the large doorway. Light streamed from the stable, the sound of voices accompanying it.

". . . dead, ma'am. Every one of them. I saw the undertaker carrying them out of the hotel just a little while ago. So now it's down to us three and you. Do you think we can handle that group by ourselves?"

Prine recognized the voice of the Preacher. His words had a cutting edge, a kind of sarcastic disdain for the lady. Prine crawled beneath the wagon, where he could observe and listen closely.

"I don't know what to do," said Priscilla Tate with despair in her voice. "Somehow this whole thing is so different than I planned it. I never thought it would be like this. I thought the threat alone would stop him, but Tom must be more dedicated than I imagined. I knew he would go far, but I never guessed anything like this!"

Prine was surprised at the familiarity with which she spoke of Stuart. He had guessed that she would know little about him, but she had talked about him as if she were well acquainted with him, calling him by his first name as if it were a natural thing. Prine was slightly unnerved. He realized that he knew very little about Thomas Stuart, and even less about Priscilla Tate.

"I think we can handle 'em alone," said one of the other men. "It's best that the others are gone—that will be that much weight off of us, so to speak. We can move quicker and easier with just us."

Priscilla burst out angrily, "How can you talk like that? You talk as if they were animals instead of men! That's what I mean when I say this thing has gotten out of hand. I would never have thought it would be like this at all—if I had I would just have let Tom have it all. Maybe that's what I should do now, before anyone else dies because of this."

There was a rather threatening silence. The Preacher rose from his seat and looked down at the distraught young girl.

"I'm afraid that's out of the question, ma'am. There's no way any of us will back out of this thing now, not this close." He shook his head. "You came into this thing mighty ignorant, lady, mighty ignorant. All that wealth is hidden out there somewhere, just like grapes ripe for the picking. Maybe you want to let someone else get hold of it, but I got no such notions. Miss Priscilla, I think maybe our use for you is finished. We can follow that bunch without your help." His hand dropped to his gun.

The girl rose from her seat and began backing away. The Preacher drew his gun and raised it slowly.

"G'bye, Miss Priscilla." He grinned as he took aim.

Prine's shot blew the gun from his hand and took two fingers with it. The Preacher cried out in pain, and Priscilla Tate darted into a stall as the other outlaws rose and drew their weapons. Prine sent a volley toward them that sent them scurrying for cover, though they managed to squeeze off several quick shots that flew harmlessly out the rear door into the night. By the time they realized where those unexpected shots had come from, Prine was gone.

He had no notions of taking on the three gunmen alone. The only thing he could do was to provide the girl with an opportunity for escape. It would be up to her to take advantage of it.

The Preacher rose from the straw-covered floor of the stable with a livid face and burning eyes. He gripped his bleeding hand and stared out the back door of the stable.

"Go after him! Kill him!"

The other two gunmen moved out the rear door, guns ready. The Preacher pulled a heavy thread from his clothes and tied it tightly around the stumps of his two blown-off fingers, cursing all the while. He tightened the threads and the bleeding stopped. He picked up his gun with his good hand and went out of the stable.

In the instant after the shot had come he had seen Prine's face. For only an instant, of course, but that was sufficient. The man's features he would not forget.

He had no doubt that the fellow was part of Tom Stuart's bunch. Yet he had not shot to kill, and that mystified the Preacher. When his time came, he himself would not be so merciful. He would find that man and make him pay with his life for the fingers he had lost.

He held the gun in his left hand, its weight more clumsy there. He moved down the alley and into the main street, searching the street for his opponent, but seeing no one who looked like him.

Then he did see Prine, who was heading into a saloon on the other end of the street. There was no sign of the other two gunmen. The Preacher holstered his gun and moved toward the saloon.

His hand throbbed; fury raged in him. He would shoot the man who maimed him, even if he had to do it right in the midst of the crowd.

Priscilla Tate rose from the stall where she had hidden. She glanced around fearfully to make sure she was alone. She was filled with questions. She too had seen for an instant the face of the man whose shot had saved her life. She recognized him as the very man who had chased her earlier that night.

She knew of the gun battle in the hotel—the same hotel on whose porch she had first noticed the man who had just now saved her. It was from that building that he had come in pursuit of her, and that was the same building that housed Thomas Stuart and his men.

So he must be a member of Stuart's group. Why had he saved her life? It was confusing, but she could not take time to clear up the mystery. She had to leave for her own safety. Her own men had turned against her. She found and saddled her horse, then mounted and moved out the back door and across the overgrown field behind it, heading for the wildland beyond. She breathed a prayer for the safety of the man who had rescued her from death. She wished she could thank him.

Prine sat in the corner of the crowded saloon, eyes fastened on the door. He didn't think any of his pursuers had seen him enter, but he could not be sure. He didn't regret firing the shot that crippled the Preacher's hand. He was glad that he had provided the threatened girl a chance to escape, and hoped that she had taken advantage of it.

The saloon was packed, people moving to and fro within it, coming between Prine and the door and cutting off his view. That made Prine uncomfortable, but again he couldn't afford to make himself obvious by craning his neck to see around the man standing in his line of vision.

But the drunk had been blocking his view for so long that Prine couldn't resist looking around him to the doorway. He was glad he did, for standing there in the door was the Preacher, who was searching the crowd over the batwing doors. Prine ducked behind the drunk again, but at that moment the fellow decided to move. The Preacher's eyes fell on Prine, and a grin came onto his face.

Prine stood and moved quickly toward the back of the saloon. The Preacher didn't even bother to push his way through the swinging doors of the front entrance as he fired three fast shots that punctured the wood of the doors and drew screams from the barmaids as it sent saloon occupants scurrying under the tables and behind the bar. But the shots missed their mark, for Prine was already gone out the back door.

The Preacher scowled and hurried through the saloon, ignoring the angry shouts of those all around him. The fat bartender rose from behind the bar with a shotgun in his hands. The Preacher fired nonchalantly in his direction with hardly a glance. The glass behind the bar shattered and the bartender ducked again.

The Preacher went out the back way after Prine. His gun felt strange in his left hand; his aim was slightly off. Where had that fellow gone? He couldn't have gotten far in the past moment.

The Preacher heard running feet in a back alley, and moved toward it. He fired a quick shot that almost nipped Prine's heel as he ran around a dark corner. The Preacher quickly darted around the same place, pausing only long enough to reload his gun. He came up on a dark alley that dead-ended into the side of another building. Prine had run himself into a trap.

But the outlaw had no time to take advantage of Prine's plight, for as soon as the Preacher showed himself around the corner, a huge cask that had sat empty in the alley came hurtling through the air to knock him in the face and send him sprawling onto his back. Then Prine leaped directly over him and darted around the corner again.

The downed man was up in a second. His gun had been knocked from his grasp, but he recovered it and took off after Prine.

He wondered where his two companions were. They had obviously lost track of Prine, but perhaps now that Prine was back in the street they would pick up his trail again. He rounded the front corner of the building, and then felt as if a club had pounded him in the face. He fell backward, then looked upward through blurred eyes to see Prine descend like a fighting mountain lion directly upon him.

The Preacher cried out involuntarily, and reached up to deflect the man falling toward him. He caught Prine's shoulders, but he could not keep Prine's rock-hard fists from pounding into his gut. His breath burst out from him, and he let go of Prine's shoulders, thus letting him fall directly on top of him.

Prine continued pounding the man's kidneys and stomach. His weight pinned the Preacher's shoulders to the earth and made it impossible for the supine man to return the blows. A crowd began to gather around the pair, whooping and laughing and calling words of encouragement to both.

The Preacher's teeth clamped down hard on Prine's left ear. The flesh of the ear was crushed between the clenching teeth. Through Prine's mind for an instant came the image of an uncle who had lost an ear in just such a manner. He had no desire to turn such occurrences into a family tradition, so he sent a particularly hard blow into the Preacher's stomach and sent the man's breath bursting from his throat with a grunt. The Preacher's teeth opened their vise-like grip momentarily.

It was just long enough for Prine to roll away, his chest heaving from exertion and his ear throbbing in pain. He felt for it. Good! The ear was still there, though it felt as if the Preacher's teeth had almost bitten clean through it.

The Preacher stood, a little slower than Prine, and the two squared off and faced each other. Both were panting, wet with sweat and covered with grime, but neither was about to quit.

The Preacher looked with hate at his opponent. He held up his right hand, the stumps from the missing fingers bleeding slightly again, and growled, "You'll pay for this with your life."

The Preacher moved quickly, amazingly fleet for a man of his size and state of fatigue, and in an instant the gun he had dropped when Prine jumped him was in his left hand. He leveled the muzzle at Prine's head.

"Now it's time to die, friend!"

The gun roared and Prine dropped suddenly to his knees. The bullet passed a mere fraction of an inch from his ear. His hand dropped to his own holster.

It was empty. In the frantic fight he had lost his weapon; he saw it on the ground several yards away, out of reach. He was left unarmed against a man who was determined to blow his head off. He dropped and rolled as the Preacher's second bullet buried itself in the dirt beside him.

He was amazed that neither shot had struck him and realized the reason for the man's poor aim—he was firing the gun with his left hand, and he was no southpaw.

Prine rose and ran straight at his foe, arms grasping toward him, and the barrel came up into his face. This is it, Prine figured. With a loud death yell he leaped toward the Preacher just as the gunman's finger squeezed down on the trigger.

The hammer clicked on a faulty cartridge, and Prine found himself pounding his fists into the face of the man whom he had expected to kill him. He felt a sudden exhilaration, and let out a whoop of joy as his fists drove the man backward.

The Preacher fell on his back, and Prine's boot caught him hard on the thigh. He yelled and rolled, and Prine moved in on him again. All about the crowd gathered once more, for it had moved back when the shots were fired, and Prine saw from the corner of his eye that he was surrounded by a circle of grinning faces.

That circle parted suddenly, and it took Prine a moment to figure out just why. Then he heard a shot. A slug ripped right into the wall beside him. He wheeled and looked wildly in the direction of the gunfire, as the Preacher fell unconscious at his feet.

It was the other two gunmen who had been in the stable with Priscilla Tate. And they were coming his way, with weapons drawn. The crowd disappeared as quickly as it had formed, like mist beneath the sun, and Prine stood transfixed for an instant in surprise.

But then he moved swiftly, darting back into the alley from which he had come shortly before. He vanished in the darkness, and he heard curses as the gunmen came after him. The roar of gunfire echoed between the walls and spurred him onward. He rounded the corner.

Where to go? Where to run? In his haste to escape Prine had run into the same dead-end alley as before. Now what could he do?

He could hear the gunmen approaching down the alley behind him. He leapt upon another empty cask and grasped the edge of the flat roof of the shed that blocked the exit of the alley. He heaved himself up onto it as the gunmen rounded the corner. Their weapons belched flames in the darkness.

He ran across the top of the structure as bullets

whistled around him. Before him rose the slightly higher wall of a barn, and an alley opened beneath him. In the barn wall facing him was an open window, slightly lower than the wall of the building upon which he stood.

He didn't even think about it as he did the instinctive thing—he dived. Straight from the shed's roof he leapt headlong, and his body arched through the open window to land on something soft.

It was a mound of hay, thick and deep. He rose up from it, looking like a straw-stuffed scarecrow, and glanced desperately around. The gunmen would be upon him in a moment, for he could hear them climbing the wall of the low building across the alley. He had no weapon with which to face them, and there seemed no good place to hide.

He heard the voices of the men as they moved across the roof, and ran quickly to the best hiding place he could find—the haystack against the opposite wall, toward the front end of the barn. Straight into it he dived, crawling to the very base of it, and heaped the hay up behind himself as best he could. He heard the scurrying of a rat close by. Apparently he had disturbed its nest. The short, stiff fur of the rodent brushed against his arm as it exited the haystack. Prine shuddered. He hated rats.

He lay silent, the hay scratching him over every inch of his body. His breath came in short, hard pants, but he tried to avoid inhaling much of the dusty atmosphere inside the haystack. Sneezing would not be advisable with two men so close by ready to kill him. He could hear them entering through the window.

"Where did he go? Did you see him?"

The other responded with a grunt. Prine heard their boots on the straw-covered dirt floor. A horse whinnied slightly in a stall.

"The door's shut. He couldn't have got out. And I swear he didn't run into the alley. He jumped right in here."

"Keep poking around. He's probably hidden some-where."

All around the barn they moved. Prine could hear them kicking stalls, opening doors, and peering into storage bins. They wouldn't stop, he knew, until they found him. They drew nearer, and it made him quite uncomfortable.

"Check up in the loft, Ben."

Feet hit the crude rungs of the ladder to the loft, and Prine heard the man moving about above. He heard the noise of hay being scattered and barrels and crates being turned over. The other man loitered below, just next to Prine's haystack. The men said little for a time; then the man below called up:

"Is there any kind of pitchfork or anything up there?"

"Yep, here's one."

"Toss it down. I want to poke through this hay."

Prine felt like a man about to be shot.

Something clattered on the floor, and Prine closed his eyes and bit his lip as, moments later, he heard the thrusting of sharp metal prongs into the hay all around him. The thrusts came again and again, each one at a slightly different place, each one getting closer to where he lay. And he couldn't move, for that would give away his location just as quickly as if he cried out. He bit his lip harder. Better a pitchfork prong than a bullet, he told himself.

Ever-closer the thrusts came, steady as a ticking clock, coming almost in rhythm with the beating of his pounding heart. Again . . . again . . .

He stifled a cry with all the willpower that was in him, for a prong of the fork had passed through the soft flesh of his calf. It had struck barely beneath the surface of his skin, but still it probed deep enough to send burning pain all through him. He hoped desperately that he had not moved when the thrust struck him. It had been only with extreme, excruciating effort that he had avoided crying out.

"Sam!" the man above cried with a note of warning to the man with the pitchfork.

The fork's thrusts stopped, and the man responded, "What is it?"

"Three men headed this way."

The man with the pitchfork stood silent for a moment, in an atmosphere of indecision. "You're right," he said.

Prine heard the descent of the one above on the ladder; then both searchers scurried toward the opposite wall and the window that opened in it. They climbed out, and Prine lay still long enough to be reasonably sure that they were indeed gone. Then he pushed his way out of the haystack.

He stood carefully on the wounded leg, testing how well it would bear his weight. The puncture wound was small. It would close and heal rapidly—that is, if he didn't come down with lockjaw or infection. He limped slightly over to the stable door.

He opened it a crack and peered into the street. Not far away he saw Ballard and the others moving down the street, their backs toward him. He knew they sought him, no doubt worried by his long absence since he had taken the body of Buster downstairs to the undertaker.

"Ballard! Over here!" Prine tried not to cry out too loudly, fearing that perhaps the gunmen were still close by.

Ballard wheeled quickly, his fast reaction betraying his nervousness. He looked very relieved when he saw Prine, and the group moved over to the barn door to join their companion.

"Prine! Are you all right? Where have you been?" Ballard sounded like a mother doting over her child, and Prine grinned.

Prine related quickly what had happened since he had carried Buster's body from the hotel room. He omitted, though, any mention of the familiarity with which Priscilla Tate had spoken of Stuart.

Stuart stood silent throughout Prine's story, but his eyes showed deep interest. Prine glanced at him, feeling uncomfortable and suspicious in his presence.

"Prine, let's get you back to that hotel and patch up your leg," said Thad. "Then let's get some sleep."

"Sounds mighty inviting," Prine said. "But first let me go see if my pistol is still where I dropped it."

It wasn't. Prine shrugged. "Well, at least I didn't lose my life. That I couldn't replace."

"Let's get back indoors," Ballard said. "This town makes me edgy."

They walked back to the hotel together.

Prine's eyes were bloodshot and red-rimmed when he rose, but he felt no desire to stay tucked away on the bed's feather mattress. He was ready to get out of Statler. He had taken his fill of the place. All of the men stirred when he rose, and moments later were up and pulling on their boots. Thad was at watch outside the door. Prine buckled on his gun belt, the pistol he had lost last night replaced by a spare Ballard had given him.

The hotel clerk refused to take their money, or even talk to them face to face. "Just leave, quickly!" he shouted from the back office where he kept his bunk. "And the next time you're in Statler, kindly stay somewhere else!"

"And a good day to you, too," muttered Ballard. Then the group headed out into the street and around back to the stable.

They really wouldn't have been too surprised to discover their horses missing, taken by some Statler horse thief. But apparently the clerk's assurances about the night watchman were accurate, for the animals were all there, looking rested and strong. They led them out of the stable and saddled them, then rode out into the street.

"Let's find a general store," said Prine. "We need to pick up a little food and a couple of lanterns. I don't want to have to stop in this town for supplies on the way back."

The store, to their chagrin, was not open, so they sat on the rough bench on the porch and waited until the storekeeper arrived. Prine wondered how the man managed to do much business in a town in which much of the populace slept in the daytime and roared all night.

The man opened his store with only a grunt of greeting to the men waiting for him. Prine and Ballard entered after him and bought some food, lanterns, and a supply of kerosene. They laid the merchandise on the counter and paid the storekeeper.

Outside they loaded the packhorses and mounted up. Then they turned their backs on the streets of Statler and headed west. It would be late evening before they reached the vicinity of Jericho Creek and the pockmarked crag of Jericho Mountain.

They fell into single file along the trail, and Ballard kept his shotgun across the saddle in front of him as he led the group. The trails were rough, and the horses had to step carefully over many roots, stumps, and boulders. The day wore on and their progress seemed slower than they had expected it would be.

Prine caught himself thinking about Priscilla Tate. Where was she now? Would she attempt to assemble a new gang in Statler? Somehow he doubted it.

Prine also pondered the general situation in which he found himself. He felt increasingly skeptical about Stuart now, full of doubt about the young man's motives. Stuart was a mysterious fellow, and Prine had always been one to want everything in the open, all cards on the table. He was suspicious that the tale Stuart had related about Priscilla Tate was not true. After all, it was only Stuart's word they had to go on that Priscilla Tate was who and what he said she was.

Prine was a man who trusted his instincts, and those said clearly that the young blond girl was no killer, and no girl who had grown up around killers. Every time he had seen her, even in that momentary glance from the Statler hotel porch, he had sensed fear in her, and worry. And even though she had shot at him in that dark, deserted building the night before, he could not feel harshly toward her. Strange, but that's how it was.

Ballard fell back from his lead position and Stuart rode out in front. Prine knew something was up when the burly rider reined up beside him.

"I think I need to talk to you, Prine."

"Don't tell me—it's about Stuart. Right?"

"On the nose. I don't like this, Prine, not one bit. There's something going on here beneath the surface. Something shady and low. That boy's got an ace that he ain't showing."

Prine glanced at the young man leading the party. "I know what you mean. I've felt it ever since he shot that prisoner yesterday. I can't prove it, of course, but I believe Stuart was lying when he said he was about to jump me. The man would have been a fool to try something like that. Stuart's a liar, and a cunning one at that."

Ballard grunted in assent. Prine could tell that his friend was thinking. "There's something that happened the other night out in the woods that I ain't told nobody," Ballard said at last.

"While Stuart was sitting watch," Ballard continued, "I was awake, but lying real still. Stuart looked us all over real close, like he wanted to make sure we were sleeping, then took off into the woods by himself. Well, I followed him, and he took off straight toward where the Tate gang was camped. I swear, it seemed like he was planning to walk right in on them. I tried to stay quiet, but he found me and got pretty upset. Then he cooled down and told me he had gone to check out a noise he had heard. I went along with the tale, but I knew he was lying. I had been awake, and there hadn't been no noise. Crazy though it may sound, I think he was planning to kill them all while the men were drunk. The girl, too, probably."

Prine said, "Why didn't you tell me about this earlier?"

"I don't rightly know, Prine. Maybe I wanted to give the boy the benefit of the doubt. But I've thought about it ever since it happened, and it's bothered me more all the time. And that's not all that's bothering me, either."

"What else you thinking about?"

Ballard was growing more intense with every word. "Prine, Stuart keeps killing men from the Tate gang who could give us information. It's almost as if he doesn't want us to know anything about the Tates. I don't understand it, and I don't like it."

Prine considered his friend's words. Ballard was right.

Stuart had effectively cut off every line of communication with the Tate gang or anyone previously involved with it.

"There's something else besides what you said, Ballard," said Prine at length. The hefty man looked at him with interest.

Prine related to him the part of the story he had left out the night before—the part about the familiarity with which Priscilla Tate had spoken of Thomas Stuart. "You know, I wasn't surprised that she knew his name, but when she spoke of him it was like she had known him well all her life. It didn't set right with me at all. She knows him far too well. According to his tale I wouldn't expect her to be on a first-name basis with him. But she called him Tom—not even Thomas—but Tom. And what's more, I—"

Prine stopped, and felt a little foolish. "Spit it out, Prine," Ballard said. "What is it?"

"It might not seem sensible to you, Ballard, but Priscilla Tate doesn't strike me as a killer. You saw her yourself the other night, and you know how out of place she seemed. And you should have heard her talking to her gang last night. She was upset by all the killing that's been going on. She wanted to back out of the whole deal! Does that sound like a killer to you? Does that sound like a hardcase daughter of one of Wesley Stoner's gang members?"

Ballard thought about it, then slowly shook his head. "No, Prine, it don't. It surely don't."

The two rode for a while longer without words. Finally Prine spoke. "What do you think we should do about it?"

"I don't know. We gave our word, and we've come this far. We've drawn blood. If Stuart isn't on the up-and-up, he'll have to tip his hand soon."

"I wish ol' Bob Stuart were here. He'd make things different."

Ballard merely grunted.

Priscilla Tate was weary and bedraggled after her all-night stay out in the wilds beyond Statler, but she couldn't rest now. Stuart's men were not far ahead, and she had to keep up with them. Had to—or this whole quest would be in vain. She slumped in the saddle and longed for a hot bath and clean clothes. But she had to stay awake and keep a sharp lookout, not only for Stuart's bunch, but also for the members of her own former gang.

The betrayal of the night before flashed yet again through her mind, and she shuddered. She had come close to death. Only the unexpected help from the man hidden beneath the wagon in the stable doorway had saved her. And the irony of it was that he was one of Stuart's men. She hadn't even been able to thank him.

His had been a brave move, one that had placed him in terrible danger, and that was in a way quite irrational. It had saved her life, but it had also put her former band of gunmen on his trail, probably more bloodthirsty than before. She had worried through the night that perhaps they had killed her benefactor, but when Stuart's group had ridden past her this morning as she lay hidden beside the trail, she had been relieved to see him with the riders, looking a little the worse for wear, but very much alive. That was good. She was grateful to him, and she didn't want to see him die.

Too many men had died already in this horrible affair, and she feared that before it was over there would be others. She felt partly responsible. She, after all, had hired the gang that had betrayed her. But what else could she have done? She couldn't let Thomas Stuart get what he sought, even though she had briefly considered that option. He had the directions to the wealth, and that was bad enough; to let him actually get that wealth was unthinkable.

But there was nothing to do but follow him. She had no idea where at Jericho Creek the treasure was hidden, and only Stuart's papers gave directions to its location. So here she was, alone and hungry on the trail, trying to stay close enough to Stuart's gang to follow it and yet also stay out of its sight.

She heard hoofbeats on the trail behind her. Not one horse, but several. Quickly she guided her horse off of the trail and into a thicket. She dismounted and grasped her derringer tightly in her slender hand.

It was the three remaining members of her former gang. They rode single file along the trail, hunched down in their saddles. They were on the trail of Stuart, just as she was. But now they were not allies but her enemies. How could she deal with two opposing groups of armed men, both of whom might kill for that treasure? It seemed hopeless.

After they passed she came out of hiding. The sun was moving toward the west, and as she mounted and moved onto the trail again it shone brilliantly into her eyes. She would have to stop for the night somewhere up ahead. This would be a night spent without even the comfort of food.

Ahead of her on the trail Prine and his group stopped for the night. Above them, illuminated from behind by the setting sun, stood the imposing peak of Jericho Mountain.

CHAPTER

17

When the light of the rising sun shone down on the rugged side of Jericho Mountain it was a magnificent sight. Prine stood and looked at it for a long time. Along the slope, and here and there across its stony surface, Prine saw dark openings: entrances to mines that had not functioned in years, and other natural openings that went into the cave system deep in the heart of the mountain. He couldn't tell which one was the entrance to the mine where the money was hidden. Stuart had been very closemouthed about specifics and had kept the packet close to him at all times.

Prine had heard descriptions of the mountain years before, back when the mines were operating. The mountain had a vast chamber in its center, at the bottom of which was an underground lake. All though the vast chasm were caves, running through the mountain like termite tunnels through old wood.

The mines often merged into these caves unexpectedly, only to return to man-made tunnels again. Many a miner had been lost in the cave system, and a few had actually plunged into the central chasm itself. Now the mountain's wealth was exhausted. Except, of course, for the wealth buried somewhere inside it by Wesley Stoner.

Only Stuart knew the exact location of that particular mine, but today he would reveal it to all of them. Prine glanced back over his shoulder toward the trail they had passed the day before. Today would be a momentous one for certain. Either he and his partners would lay their hands on that treasure, or die trying to do it.

They ate some of the food that they had purchased in Statler and Prine rolled a cigarette as Ballard bit off a chew of his tobacco. Stuart ate little. His agitation was great, and his eyes flashed with excitement. Doubts about Stuart still bothered Prine, though he too felt excited about what lay before them. But Stuart was not a man to be trusted, Prine had decided, and what would happen in that mountain no one could guess.

It was still early, but in excitement Stuart rushed things along. "Men, there's all that gold sitting up here waiting for us to take it. Let's not wait any longer to do it!"

Ballard rose ponderously, like a lazy bull. "First off you're going to have to tell us just where it is, Stuart," he said. "Just how are we supposed to locate the right entrance to that mine? The face of that mountain looks like Swiss cheese to me."

Stuart pointed off through the morning haze toward the sleepy town of Jericho Creek. "You see that church steeple over there? Well, that's our pointer. It will point right to the entrance we need, if we stand at just the right place."

"And where is that?"

Stuart reached inside his vest and drew out the packet. He carefully untied the strings holding it together and pulled out the piece of paper scrawled over with Wesley Stoner's writing. "There should be a large stone just a little to the southwest of here. If you stand on top of that stone, that church steeple points right at the entrance we need. Stoner carved his initials into the rock."

"Sounds like something out of a storybook," muttered Thad.

"I'll grant you that, but that's what the directions say," said Stuart. He was in a remarkably good humor, even better than when the group had first assembled. His enthusiasm was becoming infectious, even in spite of the disgust that the others felt toward him. Prine stirred about restlessly, anxious to get the quest under way.

"Let's go find that rock," he said.

The group broke camp and mounted, moving, with Stuart in the lead, toward the southwest. The woods were low and scrubby, though relatively thick. Rocks abounded, some rather large, but most of them small. Prine looked dismayed. How could they tell which one Stoner referred to? Surely one of the larger ones, but which?

Stuart didn't appear too disturbed about the problem, moving swiftly and surely, looking about at every sizable boulder he passed. After close to an hour of riding, though, they didn't seem anywhere near finding what they sought. Stuart turned in his saddle and looked back toward the mountain.

"We must be in the wrong place," he said. "I can't even see the tip of that church steeple from here. Let's move to the west and see what we can find."

The group moved off through the woods after Stuart. It was thicker here, and the rocks were less numerous and larger. Prine strained his eyes through the trees toward Jericho Creek. As they moved farther west, the ground sloped up slightly, and after several minutes passed, the steeple became visible again. He was encouraged.

After about thirty minutes Stuart suddenly stopped. He was gazing at an exceptionally large, tall boulder, a huge shapeless chunk of stone.

"Take a look," Ballard said.

"There—see the letters?" exclaimed Prine. "W.S. Stoner carved his initials. Let's get up there and see where that money is!"

Stuart already had leaped down and was scrambling up the rock, breathless with excitement. Thad went up after him and together they peered over the treetops toward Jericho Creek. Prine and Ballard watched the young men frown in concentration for a moment; then Thad whooped.

"We see it! It's as clear as anything! We can get there with no problem."

Stuart said, "Thad, do you see that clump of brush growing out of the side of the mountain right above the mine entrance? That'll be our landmark."

Thad nodded, and the two young men scurried back down the rock. Both mounted, and Stuart set off in the lead, eagerly heading back toward the road that led past Jericho Creek and on up the mountain. Only the top of Jericho Mountain was visible as they rode into the thicker part of the forest.

As they moved along the road Prine began to realize just how careless they had become in the last few hours. In their excitement they had virtually forgotten the threat of the men who almost certainly were tailing them. They couldn't afford to be that forgetful. Once they reached the treasure they would be facing perhaps the greatest danger yet, for the outlaw gang would have no reason to keep them alive. Once the gang knew the treasure's whereabouts they would not need Stuart's packet, nor any kind of further guidance.

They skirted around Jericho Creek. Instead of the usual facing rows of buildings, this town was spread out in a circular pattern, sitting on a sort of plateau at the base of the mountain. It was small, but fairly well inhabited, and most of the buildings were kept in good order. The men would not pass through Jericho Creek, for there was nothing for them there, and the road bypassed the town on the south.

When they reached the base of the mountain and the road began sloping gently upward, Prine became nervous. At parts of the trail they would be limned against bare rock and in clear view of anyone below. But there was nothing they could do about it.

And once they got inside that mine they would be in a very vulnerable position. It was likely that their only exit would be through the same passage they entered. And if the outlaws blocked that, there would be nothing to do but try to fight their way out, and that would be close to impossible within the confines of the mine.

The road became steeper as they ascended. The view across the town was magnificent as the sun climbed ever higher and shown down brighter on the countryside. Blue mountains lined the horizon, and the landscape was a panorama of green and purple, mixed occasionally with the gray of massive rocks that rose up here and there among the trees below.

Prine couldn't help but admire the beauty of the land, even as his eyes scanned the road for the pursuing riders he knew must be there. But no one showed himself. Prine realized that the outlaws were in good position; all they had to do was sit and wait until the money was brought out of the mine, then move in and take it. Or perhaps they would sneak into the mine while Prine and his partners were still digging it out. Either way, it would be easy for them to get that treasure.

Priscilla Tate crossed Prine's mind again. Where was she? He hoped that somewhere he had found safety. Strange, the tenderness he felt for her, Prine thought. She had actually tried to kill him, but he hadn't the slightest bit of hard feeling toward her.

After about an hour on the trail they reached the mouth of the mine. It looked much larger than Prine had anticipated, and its black depths were ominous and frightening.

Stuart was in a virtual frenzy—one that had been growing ever since that morning. Prine took note of it and cast a meaningful glance toward Ballard. Thad was dismounting.

"Someone will need to guard this entrance," Thad said. "I'll be glad to do it."

"Could be dangerous, Thad."

"This whole business is dangerous."

The group assented to Thad's request. "Keep a close eye on that road, son," Ballard instructed. "You should be able to see 'em coming, unless they find some sort of back way around the other side of the mountain. If they do that then there'll be no warning."

Prine felt a cold chill. The possibility of a back way was something he hadn't considered.

Stuart was in a tremendous hurry to get on with things. "Where are those lanterns, Prine? Let's get them lit."

Prine went over and removed the lanterns and digging tools from the back of the packhorses. Prine filled the lanterns with fuel and lit them, taking one for himself as Stuart and Ballard took the other two.

Ballard patted his son on the shoulder as he entered the dark mouth of the mine behind the others. "If there's any sign of trouble, don't try to be a hero." Thad nodded, and Ballard entered the dark cavern.

The light from the outside penetrated only a few yards into the mine, then seemed to be absorbed into the dark walls. The lanterns cast a weird glow all around them, and the dark, lonely creatures that made their home amid the crevices of the rocks and on the dank surface of the mine walls scurried away as the beams fell on them.

About a hundred feet back into the mine Prine stopped suddenly, raising his lantern and pointing to the ceiling. "My Lord, look at that!"

The ceiling of the mine was alive with bats, hanging upside down only a few feet above the heads of the men. Not a trace of rock could be seen through the dense carpet formed by the furry bodies, and their ugly faces were glaring down into the lantern light as they wrapped their leathery wings cloak-like all around them.

Without warning, the bats swarmed down and struck against the men in an effort to get outside. The men dropped to the floor; there was a mighty rush of air against them, stirred by thousands of rapidly beating winds as the multitude of bats escaped the mine.

Thad called back into the mine once the swarm had passed, and Prine assured him they were all right.

Even Stuart was a little shaken by the unexpected encounter. Prine's lantern had gone out when he dropped it to the floor, and he lit it again before the group moved on.

"This shoring looks awful weak, Prine," said Ballard. "It's about rotted out. It wouldn't take much to bring the roof down on our heads."

Prine inspected the shoring. Ballard was right—a well-placed kick could easily knock some of these beams aside.

As they progressed farther into the passage, Prine noted a slight curve in the tunnel. And off to the side opened another passage, then another, leading to dark chambers that had not seen light or life for years. Stuart had to stop several times to check the directions in the packet by the light of the lanterns before proceeding.

The air was close and thick in the cavern, heavy with a musty smell from cavern walls, that seemed to close in more with every succeeding step.

After several more turns and corners the passage widened; there was a sudden feeling of openness in the lantern-lit tunnel. There was also an increasing dampness in the air. Prine could not see what might be causing the dampness, but he felt something lay before them. They proceeded slowly, lanterns held high.

The pathway disappeared, dropping into nothingness. They had reached a central chamber. Prine held out his lantern over the depths. The light faded into blackness only a short way down into the emptiness. He kicked a loose stone over the edge. For a long time there was no sound; then, faintly, a splash echoed up from the abyss. The drop-off was sheer and maybe hundreds of feet deep.

This was a vast place, ominous and awe-inspiring. Prine felt small here, and insignificant, like an ant in a cathedral. He glanced over at his partners: Ballard's face showed awe at the deathly silence of space out before him, and Stuart's eyes glittered strangely.

The young man knelt at the edge of the abyss, and his lantern revealed a narrow ledge that wound its way along its edge to their left. He smiled and turned to the waiting men.

"This ledge leads to the spot where Wesley Stoner buried his treasure," he said.

CHAPTER
18

Prine grasped his lantern in one hand and hugged the cold stone of the wall with the other as he edged along behind Stuart on the narrow ledge, wondering all the while why he was doing such a fool thing. When he had seen how narrow and dangerous was the ledge along which they must pass, he had felt ready to throw the quest to the wind and head home. But now here he was, inching along, with a deep and dark lake hundreds of feet below, hoping the thin ledge would hold and praying that he would not lose his footing.

"The ledge widens out just ahead," Stuart gasped before him. "It should be right there that the treasure is buried in the wall."

"Just how wide does it get, Stuart?" groaned Ballard. "I hope it's wide enough for me to lie down and kiss it."

After what seemed an eternity they reached the spot. The ledge widened into a kind of natural balcony over the depths of the abyss. As each man reached it he let out a sigh of relief. Ballard was pale and panting.

"Stuart, if that money ain't here I'm not staying around to see where it is. I never have been too fond of high places."

Stuart ignored him, intent on exploring the face of the rock wall beside him. He held up his lantern, letting its beams roam over the stone. Prine looked at the young man's face. Never had he seen such an expression of fierce determination. Beads of sweat shimmered on Stuart's brow as his eyes flashed in the lantern light. And when at last the young man made out a patch on the wall of a slightly different color than the surrounding rock, he looked almost as animalistic as Buster had in the hotel room in Statler moments before Stuart killed him.

Stuart exclaimed: "Here . . . here it is! Just like the paper said! Stoner buried the money in a hole in the wall and then patched it up."

Prine hefted one of the picks. He swung the metal point into the mortar and the tip dug in, the echo resounding weirdly through the vast and hollow heart of Jericho Mountain.

Again and again the pick struck. Stuart had an eager, intense expression and seemed deeply impatient. Prine had hardly chipped away a few chunks from the mortar patch before the young man took a second pick in hand. "There's not room for both of us to dig—let me go at it for a while," he said. Stuart all but pushed Prine aside and began chopping furiously at the old mortar. Prine slipped back a little farther on the ledge and joined Ballard, who had his back against the wall. It was obvious the height had Ballard nervous.

Rapidly the patch gave way under the continual impact of Stuart's pick. His pace never slowed. When at last the pick broke through into the empty space beyond the patch, Stuart became even more frenetic, knocking away big pieces of mortar. Some fell to his feet and rolled back off the ledge to splash some seconds later into the unseen waters below.

At last Stuart threw the pick aside and reached into the black opening. He pulled out two heavy black bags wrapped in oilcloth, laughing as he did so. Prine was surprised Stuart was able to so easily heft bags that supposedly were filled with federal gold. He glanced at Ballard and read the same thought.

Stuart, trembling with excitement, knelt and began pulling the oilcloth off the bags, but abruptly he stopped. "No need," he said. "We know this has to be it."

"Mighty lightweight if it is," Ballard said. "And I never knew gold to be kept in bags before. I was expecting a strongbox."

"Forget about it," Stuart said with unexpected harshness. He glared at Ballard, sweat gleaming on his face in the lantern light. "Come on. Let's get these out of here."

Stuart picked up one of the bags. Prine took the other.

He knew at once it wasn't gold. The bag felt as if it were filled with paper.

Prine looked sternly at Stuart. "What is this?" he demanded. "It sure ain't gold, that I know."

"I will explain when we get back into the tunnel where it's safe," Stuart said, not quite as harsh with Prine as he had been with Ballard. "I assure you everything is as it should be."

Ballard started to say something, but Prine lifted his hand. No point in getting Stuart riled in so dangerous a spot as this. Once on safer ground they could explore the question fully.

Ballard, holding his lantern, went first, edging out along the ledge toward the opening to the tunnel. Stuart and Prine followed, each carrying a bag and a lantern, each walking carefully along the way.

Ballard slipped and almost fell; his lantern slid from his hand and fell over the precipice. Prine watched it arc through the blackness. It shattered on some upthrust rock far below, bursting into a flower of yellow fire that for a half second revealed the surface of the underground lake. Then the lantern splashed into the water, and the spilled coal oil burned itself quickly out on the surface of the rock.

"Ballard, you all right?"

"Fine. A horrible place to fall, that would be," Ballard said. His voice quaked a little.

"Move on!" Stuart ordered. Prine shot a hard glance at him; he didn't like Stuart's tone.

For long minutes they progressed silently. Ballard was slower now that his lantern was gone; he picked his way along carefully because he could not see the ledge ahead so clearly. At last, though, they reached the tunnel entrance and clambered to relative safety. They walked some distance, then Ballard sat heavily on the damp tunnel floor and breathed fast and deeply until he had relaxed. Prine dropped beside him, and Stuart pulled the two bags together and knelt beside them, grinning in the light of the two remaining lanterns.

"So why did you lie to us?" Prine said to Stuart.

"About the gold, you mean?" Stuart said.

"That, and whatever other wild tales you might have spun to us."

"An easy question to answer," Stuart said. He drew his pistol and pointed it between Ballard's eyes. "I lied because I needed your help to obtain two bags of cash and various valuable financial papers stolen years ago from an Omaha bank by Wesley Stoner. Given your penchant for honest dealings, I needed a tale that would allow you to help me while keeping your consciences clear. My story of stolen federal gold and the reward offered for it did the job well. Now, unfortunately for you, the job is done. Remove your pistols, slowly, and toss them away."

Prine and Ballard complied. "I knew you were rotten," Ballard said.

"Knowledge that has come too late to do you any good," Stuart said. "I'm afraid I must now dispose of you."

"How? Shoot us?"

"Oh no. No need for a murder when an accident will suffice." He flicked his glance toward the shored-up mine roof. "These timbers give away and this place would collapse. An unfortunate but predictable accident in an old mine. I'll let you perform the honors of using your pick on the shoring beams, Prine. If you don't, I'll shoot your friend here between the eyes, like the pig he is."

"And what about Thad? How will you dispose of him so neatly?" Prine asked.

"Not your concern," Stuart said. "I'll deal with him after you're gone."

"What about protection? You need it worse now than ever," Prine said. "You can't afford to get rid of us now."

"I can't very well afford to leave you alive, can I? You're right—I do need protection. I'll just have to be careful until I can buy some of it. Certainly I've got enough money to do that now."

"Priscilla Tate's old gang members will be out there, looking for you. They may be coming up the mountain right now."

"I'm aware of my difficulties," Stuart snapped. "My plan may not have been perfect, but so far it's kept me alive and gotten me what I wanted. Now, get up. Ballard, you stand against that wall. Prine, take that pick and knock out the shoring beam."

Prine felt a burst of fury, and as he stood, lunged a bit at Stuart. But he pulled up short, for he knew Stuart truly would kill Ballard.

"The pick, Prine."

A few moments later, Stuart was slowly backing away from the area, the pistol still raised, and Prine was poised at a shoring beam, pick ready. He looked at the beam, at the cracked tunnel ceiling above it, and hoped Stuart was wrong. Maybe the mine would hold up without the old beams. Yet he doubted it.

"Good-bye, Prine, and thank you," Stuart said. "Knock away the beam."

"We'll survive this, Stuart. We'll find a way out and track you down."

"I doubt it. Now do the job. I have no more time to waste."

Prine closed his eyes, took a breath, and swung the pick. The beam shifted. A terrible groaning, crackling noise filled the tunnel—the sound of loose rock shifting.

"Again!" Stuart commanded, still backing away.

Prine lifted the pick again and swung. This time the beam fell away completely. The crackling noise became far louder. Prine ran back toward Ballard.

Stuart wheeled and began to run as the first small pieces of rock showered down.

CHAPTER
19

A burst of gunfire echoed down from the entrance of the mine. Stuart stopped and swore as the noise of running feet and blasting guns came ever closer, echoing loudly through the mine.

Stuart had forgotten Prine and Ballard for an instant, and as he turned his back on them, both men recovered their guns. More blasting gunfire reverberated through the tunnel.

It could only mean one thing: Thad had been surprised by the remaining members of the former Tate gang. Prine remembered Ballard's warning about a possible back way up the mountain.

Stuart let fly a long string of oaths as Thad ran into view. Prine heard voices and men running into the tunnel.

Thad took no notice of Stuart, ignorant of his treachery, and there was certainly no time for him to be told with both the threat of a cave-in and death by outlaw gunfire hanging over them all. The only thing they could do right now was to try to move back far enough to escape the tons of rock that would come crashing down within seconds.

"Tate gang . . . came at me from behind . . ."

The flickering lantern light illuminated three gunmen moving at a run straight back toward them. Prine recognized the face of the Preacher by the glow of the kerosene flame.

Stuart came out of his daze, grabbing one of the lanterns as he moved back farther in the passage. Prine grabbed the other, then sent two quick shots at the intruders and scrambled after Stuart as bullets kicked up chips of stone at his feet.

The three gunmen came on, their shots more carefully placed now, and the Preacher obviously making for Prine. Prine's foot struck a small boulder that lay in the passage, and his body pitched to the side just as the remaining strained shoring at last gave up its burden and collapsed.

Stone and dust, choking, stinging, pounding into flesh like a horrible hammer blow, filling the eyes, nose, blinding, hurting. The ominous rumbling had become a roar that sounded as if the very mountain itself were groaning in pain as a portion of its matter broke away. Prine didn't realize until it was over that mixed in with the noise of the crumbling stone was his own cry. Then suddenly it was done, and he was aware of nothing but being in a small chamber of stone, breathing a dust-filled atmosphere, and seeing a strange, flickering glow.

He raised himself, painfully, and looked about. He had been thrown aside by the falling rock, pushed into this side chamber like a feather before the wind. And the dim light came from the lantern he had held, now half-buried in dirt and rubble, its flame growing steadily lower.

His gun—where was his gun? He felt for it, straining his dust-filled eyes to see it, but could not find it. He half-rose again, failed, then tried once more, this time making it all the way to his feet. And he stared groggily ahead, somehow not even surprised to see a man standing before him with a .44 leveled at his gut.

The Preacher. Prine stared at him almost stupidly. The outlaw was disheveled, coated with dust, and blood trickled down from a wound in his scalp, but there was a grin on his face. He let loose a sort of low laugh before he spoke.

"Well, friend, it looks like it's me and you again, doesn't it? This time I'm going to kill you . . . you won't escape me now." He raised the gun and leveled it at Prine's forehead. Prine rather groggily recognized the weapon as his own.

He dropped and rolled as the Preacher fired, the blast intensely loud in the small chamber. Prine's entire body was stung by tiny pieces of something that blasted into the rock all around him, and the Preacher let out a cry of anguish almost at the same time he fired the shot.

Prine rose to see the man grasping at a bleeding hand. The shattered handgun lay on the ground before him. Its barrel was shredded, splintered, and as Prine's mind began to clear, he realized what had happened.

The gun's barrel had apparently been choked with grit and rubble during the cave-in. The Preacher's shot had turned the weapon into a miniature bomb that had maimed his good hand and sent forth the shower of grit that had stung Prine a second before.

The lantern died away into a dull red. Prine feared it would go out. Without a moment's hesitation he attacked.

His hands closed around a throat as thick and stout as a young oak. Immediately the Preacher's hand struck his jaw, and he was knocked away, the salty taste of blood in his mouth. Whether it was his own blood or that of the Preacher he could not tell. He fell back, his gripping hands shredding his opponent's shirt and dragging him down on top of him.

A bloody hand pounded Prine's face, but he ignored the pain and shoved the heavy man off of him with strength he didn't know he possessed. A primitive feeling flowed through him, as if this weird battle by lantern light had turned him from a man to a beast. He struck his opponent with a viciousness he had never known before, and the blows that were returned were every bit as fierce. This would be a battle to the death, he knew deep inside, and he almost welcomed it. He rained down more blows with ever-increasing force.

Then the Preacher was gone. Prine wheeled, his arms out and his fists clenched, and listened. Where was he? He heard gasping breaths, but he couldn't tell where they came from. Then something hard struck his head with a grazing blow, and he fell.

He was dazed again, his head throbbing and his senses reeling. He realized what had happened: The Preacher had thrown a large stone, striking him cruelly. Had the blow been a little more direct, it probably would have killed him. Instead, it had only grazed his head, but that was bad enough, for he was stunned now, and down, ready for the

Preacher to finish him off. He writhed on the rough stone floor, and heavy kicks began pounding him. Prine's mind raced toward senselessness.

With the last effort he could muster, he reached out blindly in the darkness, and his hand closed by sheer chance on the Preacher's ankle. Suddenly the man was falling, landing atop him, then sliding away over him into a void directly beside Prine. A hand closed on Prine's shirt, pulling him after the falling outlaw, drawing him too toward a pit that the Preacher had fallen into, a pit that neither had known was there, and which opened for hundreds of feet straight down. Prine heard the Preacher's pitiful cries as he dangled for a moment over the black hole, then his scream as he plunged far, far into the blackness, deep into the very roots of the mountain. Prine almost went senseless, his body dangling half into the hole, teetering on the very edge as if undecided whether or not to fall. Unconsciousness threatened to engulf him.

He awoke in a soft but brighter glow, a hazy light from an origin he could not ascertain. A soft hand stroked his brow. His eyes focused slowly, and he realized that he was lying on his back in the same chamber as before, and the hand was that of a young lady. He squinted and looked into the face above him. Confusion swept over him.

"Pri—Priscilla . . . " His voice failed him before he could say the whole name.

. "You know me? How?" Her pretty face showed her surprise. Then it returned to its former expression: one of concern, tenderness. "I guess Tom must have told you. But now isn't the time to worry about that. You were almost gone, you know—almost into that pit. I got the lantern up again and pulled you away from the edge. You saved my life once. Now I've returned the favor." Her voice was soft and her hand stroked his brow almost lovingly. "I'm glad I had the chance. It was a way of thanking you."

Prine's rationality began to return slowly, and the scattered pieces of the jigsaw puzzle of the last moments began to put themselves together. He realized what had happened; how the Preacher had knocked him to the ground beside the natural well farther back in the chamber, how his own hand had unbalanced the Preacher and sent him hurtling into the dark hole to his death at the bottom far below. Priscilla Tate, had obviously managed to sneak past Thad and follow them into the mine. And it had been she who had pulled him from the brink of the pit. Priscilla Tate had saved his life. Even in his still-groggy state the irony of it was not lost upon him.

He sat up, looking into her face. "But we're supposed to be enemies . . . why?" Prine asked.

"I don't know who is my enemy and who is not. All I know is that we're trapped together here and if we don't stick together we'll never get out. You saved my life and I've saved yours. You don't seem like an enemy to me."

Prine paused in thought. "And you don't seem like an enemy to me." Then into his mind came something he had forgotten in the confusion of the last moments: Ballard, Thad, the cave-in.

Prine leapt up. "Ballard! He was out there when the roof caved in! And Thad!"

Priscilla stood. "The others? I don't know what happened to them."

"Hush!" Prine said, a little more sharply than he intended. "Listen!"

They stood quietly, trying not to breathe.

It was faint and muffled, but it was an unmistakable noise: gunfire, coming from the other side of the rubble heap. Someone was alive out there after all, apparently several people, for that was a sizable gun battle they were listening to. So even if they got out of this chamber, which itself seemed impossible, the danger would not be over.

Prine said, "Give me that lantern."

She handed him the lantern, and he began a close and hurried inspection of the pile of boulders. She looked on too, and her heart sank. It seemed like an impenetrable mass, a hopelessly thick barrier to escape. It began to dawn on her what being trapped here would mean. Slow death, thirst, hunger—she tried to block out the thoughts.

Prine scrambled up onto the heap, his lantern held aloft and his free hand probing into the crevices of the rocks, trying to move them aside and make some sort of passage that would accommodate them. But he was having no luck, for in spite of his efforts the huge boulders remained immobile. He continued for long minutes, moving all over the face of the rock mass, trying to move every small boulder. It looked hopeless.

In a sort of desperate gesture Prine heaved hard on one last boulder, and was surprised when the rock gave way. It exposed an opening blocked with small stones. Prine smiled.

"Here, hold the lantern. I think I can dig our way through here." He began moving the stones, making a sort of tunnel through the rubble, burrowing like a human mole. And as he knocked more and more rock aside, the sound of the gunfire grew louder from the other side of the stone.

With a groan and heave Prine broke through the barrier. And at the same moment he realized that but for his knife he was unarmed.

CHAPTER

20

Prine looked out of the narrow opening he had made into a scene out of hell. There was a dim light in the main passage of the mine, the same flickering lantern light as before. The atmosphere was dusty and it was difficult to see. Occasional flares of light exploded sporadically from various places around the mine, accompanied by loud, echoing blasts and the sound of ricocheting bullets. How many people in the mine had survived the cave-in Prine couldn't tell.

Prine stayed far enough back in his little tunnel to remain safe from flying bullets, and studied the tons of earth and stone that blocked the main entrance to the mine. He could see no opening at all. Apparently the collapse had completely blocked the way out of the mine. Whether friend or enemy, all in the mine had one thing in common: They were most definitely trapped.

Prine longed for a gun.

He prayed fervently that Ballard was still alive. He couldn't bear to think that he had died beneath the crushing stones.

Priscilla's voice reached him from behind. "What can you see out there?"

Prine inched along backward until he stood beside her in the small chamber again. "I can't see much, and I'm not sure who's out there. But it must be some of my friends and your old friends, or else they wouldn't be shooting at each other." He suddenly recalled the treachery of Stuart, and realized that the statement he had just made might not

110

necessarily be true. Even if the former Tate gang members had been killed, it was possible that Ballard and Thad were still alive out there, fighting it out with Stuart. Or Stuart might be fighting the outlaws.

"Priscilla, you stay here until it's over. There's no point in you risking your life." He paused, unsure of what he wanted to say. "I'm glad I met you, ma'am, and I'm grateful for what you did for me. I'm sorry we had to be on opposite sides in all this. The name's Jeremy Prine, ma'am. I'll be going."

He climbed up on the rocks again, scrambling up into his escape tunnel, an unarmed man going out to try to help friends even though he didn't know where they were or what he could do for them.

Priscilla noticed that the gleaming lantern light flashed on something in the corner. It was the derringer she had lost when the mine collapsed, almost hidden in the dust. She ran toward it, picking it up and inspecting it for damage. Everything appeared in working order. She brushed the dust from it.

Here was a weapon for Jeremy Prine—not a good one, certainly, but better than nothing. She ran to the small crawlway he had entered a moment before and looked into it just in time to see him slip out on the other side. She thought of calling to him, but the fear that her cry might draw dangerous attention to the unarmed man stopped her. He was out there, right in the thick of battle, with no weapon but a knife to aid him.

Prine felt like a shooting-gallery target as soon as he dropped from the passage onto the rubble heap and down to the floor of the mine. The lantern light was dim, hardly sufficient illumination for a chamber of this size, and the only other source of light were the flashes of gunfire that burst from various portions of the passage. He noticed that the crack of a particular gun would come from first one spot, then another. These men were moving about as they fought, and that made things pretty confusing.

So far no one had taken a shot at him, and he was surprised at that. He could see the areas where the opposing sides were holed up, but who was a friend and who was an enemy he could not tell.

There was also no way to remain standing where he was, a clear target for whoever might first decide to take a shot at him. He had to move somewhere. He glanced around to his left.

Two quick bursts of gunfire came from behind a pile of dirt, rocks, and old shoring wood. The flash of the blasts illuminated the face behind the gun for only an instant, but that was sufficient. It was Ballard.

Prine ran toward the spot, hoping he wouldn't spook Ballard by his sudden appearance and maybe risk taking a bullet from his friend. He made a headlong dive over the rock pile, landing in a heap beside his hefty partner.

"Prine—where have you been? I thought you died under the rocks!"

"No, sir, Ballard. I wouldn't think of doing a thing like that. But I did manage to lose that gun you loaned me. You got another?"

Ballard's answer was a grunt and a gesture to their left. Prine gasped when he saw the body of Thad lying there very still, hardly breathing, it seemed. His face was pale, and dark blood stained his features.

"What was it, Ballard—a bullet?"

Ballard squeezed off another shot as he nodded. "It just grazed his head, I think, but it put him out colder than a light. You can use his gun."

Prine took the young man's weapon, a Colt, and spun the chamber. It was fully loaded. He started to rise to fire, then realized that he didn't know where the enemy was—and based on the ambiguous standing of Stuart right now, even who the enemy was.

"Who are we fighting, Ballard? Is Stuart with us or against us?"

"He sure ain't with us, Prine. Only one of them outlaws survived that cave-in, and he's holed up to the left, back toward the tail end of the mine. Stuart's over there about straight in front of us, and he's taking on the whole lot of the rest of us. This is a three-way fight."

"What about the money?"

"Stuart's got it."

Prine glanced up over the pile long enough to see Stuart duck back down behind a boulder that apparently had been tossed to its resting place by the force of the cave-in. He readied his gun for Stuart's next appearance, and when the young man again thrust his head up, Prine let loose with a shot that almost scalped him. Stuart ducked again.

"I'm back, Stuart! You're fighting me and Ballard together now!" The words were a warning, a challenge. It felt good to say them.

Stuart gave no answer, save for two well-placed shots that actually clipped off some of Prine's hair when next he showed himself. Then came another burst of fire from the back of the mine, smacking all around him and Ballard. The gunman apparently sent a slug Stuart's way, too. But the bullets struck harmlessly on all sides. Prine realized this was a battle that could go on for quite some time. The thing that would end this fight would be when one side ran out of ammunition.

Quickly he assessed their situation. He had a handful of cartridges in his pocket, and Thad's gun belt was circled with others. With Ballard's supply they should be able to fight for some time yet.

The outlaw moved at the back portion of the passage, and they concentrated attention on that area. The lantern light was dim, but still they could make out the shadowy form of the man as he ran from his hiding place toward the other side of the tunnel. What prompted the man to move Prine could not guess; maybe he was running low on ammunition and wanted to find a better vantage point. But it was a fatal move, for Stuart's gun spoke out three times, loudly, and the man fell to the floor of the mine, a corpse before his last breath was out of his lungs.

For a long time there was silence. The smell of spent gunpowder hung in the air, and the dimly lit chamber was choked with dust and smoke. Stuart spoke first: "Well, gentlemen, it looks like it's down to you and me again. I was certainly sorry to have to kill your son, Ballard."

"You didn't kill him."

Stuart laughed. "Well! I'm not quite the shot I thought! But no matter—I'll take care of him later. Now, throw your weapons over the rock pile and onto the floor where I can see them."

Prine laughed. "You seem to forget that there's two of us and one of you. It seems to me that you're the one who should toss over your gun, boy. You got nothing to back up your bluff!"

"Tom!"

The feminine voice echoed in the mine. Prine frowned. The girl had done the very thing he had told her not to do.

Ballard looked confused, but Prine had no time to explain. Stuart laughed derisively on the other side of the passage. Prine looked over the rock pile. Priscilla was standing there, her back toward him, and in her hand was a derringer. Her trembling fingers betrayed her fear.

"Well, Priscilla! What a surprise!" Stuart said. "What do you want of me?"

"I want you to give up, Tom."

"Priscilla—don't be a fool! He'll kill you!" Prine shouted.

"I'm sorry, Mr. Prine. This is something I have to do. This man was the death of my father, and I intend to see him pay."

Prine knew the girl was in danger, and he had to intervene. But before he had made it halfway over the rock pile, the roar of Stuart's .44 filled the mine, and Priscilla screamed. Prine went over the pile and toward her just as Stuart came out of his hiding place to grasp her around the neck and place the barrel of his gun to her head. Then he wheeled so that he stood behind her. His gun was firmly pressed against her temple.

Prine stopped in his tracks. He saw the girl's derringer on the floor of the mine far out of reach, its barrel shattered by Stuart's last shot.

"Don't move another step, Prine. If you do I'll kill her. You know I'm not bluffing."

"Yes, Stuart, I know."

"Prine, what's going on here?" Ballard asked with exasperation.

"I'll explain later, Ballard," said Prine. "Right now let's just take it real easy, real easy."

"That's right, Prine. You're smarter than I gave you credit for," said Stuart. "Now you just step back and get rid of your gun—you too, Ballard—and I'm going to take this young lady toward the back of this mine again. I think I may have seen a way out of here. If you make the slightest move, I swear I'll kill her, and you too. C'mon! Drop those guns!"

Prine's weapon clattered to the floor. With more hesitation, Ballard too yielded up his gun, then stood with hands raised. "That satisfy you, Stuart?"

"Very much so. Now, you gentlemen stand aside while I collect my money." He kept the gun on Priscilla's temple as he picked up the box and hefted it under his arm. Then he shoved her along as he moved over to where the lantern sat. He picked it up and held it before him, not caring that the hot metal occasionally swung into his lovely prisoner, burning her.

Then he was off, moving toward the rear of the mine, the lantern light fading, leaving Prine and Ballard in darkness. Neither moved for a time, then Ballard said, "Well, what are we going to do?"

"Help her," Prine said. "It appears to me that we've been helping out the wrong one so far." He struck a match and held it aloft for light.

"That's for certain. But what can we do? If he sees us he'll kill her, and us too. I'm surprised he didn't shoot us just now." Suddenly he paused, then said, "C'mon—there's not a second to lose. Our friend Stuart isn't the threat we think he is. Let's go!"

"What . . . but . . . " Prine's protests were no use. Ballard was already heading down the passage, feeling along like a blind man. Prine shrugged and followed him, hoping that whatever he had in mind would work. He certainly couldn't guess what it might be.

After a few moments of blind scrambling, they saw the light of Stuart's lantern moving along before them. They were almost to the end of the mine, where the passage opened into the massive central chamber. Unless Stuart was planning on moving out on the ledges again, he would be forced to stop.

21

As the two approached Stuart, they slowed, trying to remain silent as they drew steadily nearer. Stuart still held Priscilla, the gun pressed against her head. He was moving fast, obviously trying to reach the central chamber as quickly as possible. But why? He had mentioned an escape route, but what route could possibly open from that vast chasm filled with cold water?

The light from the lantern Stuart clutched cast a weird glow all about him.

Prine wondered what Ballard's plan was. How could he hope to stand up unarmed against a desperate man with a hostage and a .44 in his hand?

Stuart had reached the very end of the mine now, standing on the brink of the chasm, and he had an expression of uncertainty on his face. Priscilla looked frightened, but there was dignity in her bearing, and a defiance that would not be masked by her fear. It was obvious that she would face death bravely if it came to that. Prine admired her in the midst of his apprehensions. He still knew next to nothing about her; what information Stuart had given them probably had been fabricated. But nevertheless he felt she should be defended. His mind flashed back to the night he had first seen her in her camp, gun in hand and that same expression of fear on her face.

Ballard had stopped now, and Prine halted beside him. Prine had a sense of helplessness to which he was very unaccustomed. The next few minutes were to be crucial ones, and he wondered what his role in them was going to be.

Stuart still loitered nervously at the brink of the chasm, the image of insecurity. It was a singular way for him to act, Prine mused, for it seemed that if anyone had the upper hand in this situation it was he. What could he be afraid of?

"Stuart!"

The young man jumped, a low cry coming from his throat. His eyes were open wide, fearful. From his reaction to Ballard's voice, one would have suspected he had been stabbed with a needle. Prine glanced over at Ballard, who strode slowly yet confidently toward the young man and his hostage.

"What's the matter, boy? Didn't you expect to see us again? Did you think we'd cower back there in the dark while you walked out of here with that money and the young lady? Surely you didn't think that, now did you, Stuart?"

"You stay back! I swear I'll kill you—and her first! I swear to God I will!"

My Lord, Prine thought, the fellow's panicked! What had happened to the confident fellow of moments before? There was no logical reason for it, as long as he held that gun in his hand—unless that gun was not as threatening as it seemed.

As Ballard laughed at the frightened young man, Prine realized what his friend had thought of moments before back in the blackness of the mine. Before the cave-in Stuart had been ready to kill them, and the only reason he had not shot at them was so Thad would not grow suspicious outside the mouth of the mine. But that consideration was meaningless now; Thad was back in the darkness, unconscious.

Yet Stuart had not shot them back there when he took Priscilla as his prisoner. Why? Why hadn't he just finished them off then and there and been through with it?

There could only be one answer—his gun was empty. His threat on the life of the girl, and their lives as well, was a bluff. Ballard was calling that bluff, and apparently thoroughly enjoying doing it. Prine smiled as the big man moved forward.

"Well, c'mon, Stuart—kill me! Why are you waiting? You said you would kill me, but I don't see you doing anything about it."

Stuart retreated steadily backward until he stood close to the edge of the precipice. He stopped then, the bags of money dropping to the earth, and with a final threat tried to stop Ballard's approach.

"Stop right there, fat man. One more step and I'll throw her over."

But Priscilla lunged forward and away. She tripped, though, and fell against Ballard, knocking them both to the ground.

Stuart cursed loudly and came forward. Priscilla rolled off to the left, but before Ballard was half-risen, Stuart planted a firm kick right in his side, sending him sprawling again.

Prine's knife came out of his belt, and with a shout he approached Ballard's antagonist. But before Prine could reach him, Stuart's boot came up again, striking Prine's wrist forcefully, and the knife flew from his grasp to clatter onto the floor, spin across, and drop into the chasm.

Stuart picked up a large rock, and as his left fist pounded hard into Prine's gut, the stone bashed the side of his head. Prine went down, stunned once more, out of the fight for good. As Priscilla rushed to Prine's side, Stuart turned to take on Ballard again, who had by now risen haltingly to his feet.

Stuart rushed straight into his arms. The big man managed to land one blow before Stuart tore into him like a Kansas tornado, bloodying his face, bruising his gut, sending his head spinning with blow after blow. Ballard had not anticipated such strength, and with Prine out of the battle, he felt a moment of doubt as to whether he would make it through this alive. But he growled like a grizzly and shoved his weight forward, pushing Stuart backward into the wall.

Ballard then spun away, breathless and dizzy, trying to buy time for himself before the young and energetic fighter was on him again. But it was no use, for Stuart bounded back from the wall and again pounded Ballard's jaw.

Priscilla watched the eerie, lantern-lit battle in desperation. She felt helpless, alone, now that Prine lay stunned with his head in her lap. Everything depended on Ballard's ability to overcome Stuart. Should Stuart come out victorious, it would mean death for all of them.

Prine stirred, moaned, and she looked down into his face. He wasn't unconscious, at least not totally, but could he recover in time to save Ballard's life? She prayed he would, yet growing in her mind was the frightening conviction that if anyone was to save them, she would have to be the one.

Stuart had the money bags in his hand, and swung them hard at Ballard, catching him in the side, sending him reeling away to teeter perilously on the brink of the black abyss, his hands waving wildly about as if to grasp a handhold in the air.

Then, in tandem with Priscilla's scream, he fell.

Stuart laughed as the bulky man dropped into the darkness. Ballard groped and his hands clutched the side of the precipice, holding on until his knuckles were white. He swung out over two hundred feet of emptiness, only his straining fingers keeping him from certain death.

Stuart walked casually over to where the big man clung to the stone, looking over at him with a smile on his face.

"Hey, fat man—where's your smart mouth now? You can't imagine how much pleasure this is going to give me." He hefted up the money bags for Ballard to see. "Thanks for your help in getting this, old man. I'll build a monument in your memory."

Slowly Stuart's boot came up, his movements cool and deliberate so that his victim could see exactly what was coming. Then slowly his foot began its descent. Ballard closed his eyes.

Prine stirred alone in the darkness, rose, and looked about with foggy eyes. His mind was blank, but he felt distressful, as if he had just had a nightmare he couldn't quite remember. He shook his head violently, trying to clear away the cobwebs from his mind and the blur from his vision.

He remembered it all in a horrible rush. He jerked upright, noticing several things at once.

Stuart stood at the edge of the precipice, his boot

pressing down hard on something, again and again. Ballard was nowhere to be seen, but Priscilla was up, moving rapidly toward the young man, who stood with the money bags still slung over his shoulder and laughing like a playing child as he continued pressing with his boot. Just as Priscilla rushed at him, Prine saw out of the corner of his eye a figure staggering in from the dark mine passage, with bloody head and stumbling feet.

Prine saw what Priscilla was trying to do, but also that she would fail, for even as she drew near Stuart saw her. He wheeled, stepping off Ballard's hands for a moment, and stiff-armed Priscilla in the face. She fell, knocked down by the force of her own run. Stuart laughed, but the laugh choked away as Ballard's right hand came up and closed around his ankle. Stuart, frozen with horror, looked down at Ballard with wide eyes.

"Good-bye, boy," Ballard said as he pulled out and down.

Stuart jerked forward and almost caught himself before the weight of the money bags shifted forward, throwing him out headlong over the precipice, sending his body arching over Ballard to fall screaming for long seconds into the emptiness, his hands never losing their grip on the bags of money.

Even after the noise of the splash had reached the ears of those on the brink of the chasm, the scream echoed for many moments.

Prine was up now. Quickly he moved over beside Priscilla Tate, who stood weeping, and pulled her back from the brink of the abyss. Then the figure he had seen moving out of the darkness came up beside him. It was Thad, weak and pale.

Without a word Prine and Thad went to where Ballard clung with weakening fingers to the rock. They grasped his wrists, his massive weight threatening to drag them after him to the dark water below. With straining muscles the two men heaved, their task made all the harder by their weakened condition. But slowly Ballard moved upward, his face pale but his eyes reflecting determination to reach safety. Straining, Thad and Prine managed to pull his hefty form up onto the rocks, and he moved at a crouch back as far as he could from the chasm to collapse on the mine floor in a silent, gasping heap.

Prine and Thad moved slowly away from the opening, but not before Prine looked down into the depths that had swallowed Stuart. For several moments he looked, then spoke: "Rest in peace, Thomas Stuart. You have your treasure now."

It was all so ironic Prine couldn't hold back a shudder. He moved away from the brink and sat down beside Priscilla. It was a long time before anyone broke the silence.

Ballard finally spoke. "Prine, if he had only let go of that money, he might not have fallen. But he wouldn't let go, not even for his life."

Prine shook his head. "I think that money *was* his life, Ballard. I think it's the only thing he lived for. In a way I'm glad it's gone. All that money has brought is death."

Thad spoke groggily. "Would someone fill me in on what has happened? It's all pretty hazy."

Prine told of the fight between him and the Preacher in the side passage right after the cave-in and of the role of Priscilla in the whole affair. Ballard eyed the girl closely, impressed by her bravery, and Thad looked at her with a different sort of expression. For several minutes Prine told his side of the story, though he too wanted information from the others to fill in the gaps he couldn't.

So after he was finished, Ballard took over, giving all the information he had, further piecing together the story. Then the men in the lantern-lit passage looked toward the girl.

"Ma'am, it looks like you're the only one we don't know much about. Stuart told us that you were the daughter of one of Wesley Stoner's gang members, a man named Tate. I don't hardly believe that anymore," Prine said. "Would you care to fill us in? I'm a bit curious to know."

The girl nodded. "Mr. Prine, I think you'll be surprised at what I have to say. But before I tell you about me, let me set you straight on Thomas Stuart. I'm sure he didn't tell you what he really is."

"He said he was the son of Bob Stuart, an old partner of ours from the war," Prine said. Then briefly he told her the story Stuart had related of how Bob Stuart had come by the packet. Priscilla appeared sometimes disturbed, sometimes infuriated by what she heard.

"There's more truth in his tale than I would expect," she said. "But not nearly enough for you to really understand what Tom was. It was true that he was the son of Bob Stuart, but he was illegitimate, the son of a prostitute, the accidental offspring of an unfortunate set of circumstances that haunted his father for years afterward. Bob Stuart supported his son, for he was not a man to shirk responsibility, and in a way I think he really loved the boy. But he never told his wife of him, in spite of the fact that he was conceived before he married her, and he hired a woman in a town not too far away to raise him. He would visit Tom a lot, telling him stories of his past, his days in the war—that's why Tom knew of you—but still the boy never returned his love. Maybe he resented not being allowed in the family, and the fact that he was not mentioned in the will. Bob Stuart had made provisions for his son other than the official will, but that didn't seem to matter. As the boy grew he came to hate his father, and to plague him constantly."

Prine interrupted. "Begging your pardon, ma'am, but just how do you know all of this? Who are you?"

"Because my name is not Tate. My name is Priscilla Stuart, and Bob Stuart was my father."

Priscilla's pronouncement brought a stunned silence to the men. Yet even as he sat dumbfounded, Prine could see a bit of family resemblance in her face, and suddenly he realized why he had felt such a strange tenderness for her. She reminded him of his old friend.

"But that isn't the whole story, gentlemen," Priscilla continued after her words had sunk in. "Let me give you the background of that packet that Tom carried, as well as a little history about his relationship to my family.

"While my mother never knew of Tom's existence at all, Father told me at a very young age, as soon as he thought I was grown enough to understand what he was saying, as well as the need to keep it all a secret from Mother. I'm not sure just why he told me; maybe he needed to let out the secret to someone just to clear his mind. The guilt of having an illegitimate child really bore on him, aging him more quickly than he would have otherwise. But that's not what's important here.

"I actually grew quite close to Tom during my younger years, for my father would often let us play together while we were still children. Tom had not yet become the kind of individual he finally became, though in retrospect I can see that the roots of his bitterness toward my father were growing even then. We were very close playmates, though our time together was greatly limited, since we could only see each other when my mother wasn't around. But my father showered us both with love . . . well, I'm not sure he exactly loved Tom, but he certainly cared for him. We were happy.

"But as Tom grew older his bitterness increased, as did his wildness. He grew to be a source of grief to my father, and Father's inability to share that grief with my mother only compounded his troubles. When Tom had grown to be a young man, he realized the hold he had over my father, and threatened to expose the truth to my mother if he didn't receive a sizable bit of money. My father gave in to his demands, over my objections, and Tom was satisfied . . . for a time.

"I was infuriated at the way in which he used my father, especially after the way he had been given so many privileges while growing up. I begged Father to go ahead and confess the whole affair to Mother, telling him that she was strong enough to take it, but he wouldn't hear of it. So things went on pretty much the same.

"Then Tom began gambling, running up huge debts, and his demands on my father increased steadily. It was growing almost impossible to satisfy those demands without making Mother grow suspicious, but somehow Father managed to do it. He made a lot of sacrifices just to keep Tom's mouth shut.

"All the while I grew to resent Tom more and more. I longed to do something to stop him; I even dreamed of killing him, but it was all just a fantasy. But when I saw what he was doing to my father, it really hurt me. And things just got worse and worse.

"Then came Father's encounter with Wesley Stoner out in the woods near our farm. Stoner was dying, and told Father of the hidden money—a way of clearing a black conscience, I believe. Father had no plan to do anything but report the incident, but before he could, Tom came around again, demanding far more money than ever before. And for once my father stood up to him, refusing him. I think his rage had built to the point that he could stand no more. Tom grew violent—it's not something I like to talk, or even think, about—and killed my father, murdered him in cold blood right in front of my eyes. I don't think he really intended to do it, for it was like cutting off his money supply, but his fury got the best of him. Later he seemed to have no real remorse about it at all, except to say that he was sorry he couldn't get more money out of the old fellow.

"Then he began talking about Mother, saying that if I didn't provide him with some cash, he would reveal himself to her, even dump Father's body down in front of her. I knew that something like that would be far too much for her to take, so I gave him Stoner's packet, and told him how my father had come by it.

"I fabricated a story about a robber to explain the murder of my father. My mother was heartbroken; it was much harder on her even than you might imagine. She lived for Father—he was her very life.

"After Father was buried, Mother became ill. She died within two weeks of his murder, and we buried her beside him.

"Then I grew very obsessed with stopping Tom, and I'm afraid I did some pretty rash things. I came west, and began frequenting saloons and similar places in order to pick up a gang of men hardy enough to stop Tom. He learned of what I was doing and gathered you men for protection.

"Members of my gang began betraying me soon after I was on Tom's trail, and going off on their own after Tom. My last three gang members turned against me in Statler. If you hadn't fired that shot, Mr. Prine—I hate to think what would have happened.

"After that, I still couldn't give up on my plans, so I came after you alone. I followed from a distance, knowing all the while that my former gang members were following too, and I managed to slip into this mine while your sentry was tending your horses. I hid in that side passage, planning to follow you out and try to get that money somehow.

"Now it looks like my quest is over. Tom is dead, and that money is gone forever. In a way that's best, I guess."

Ballard shook his head slowly as the narrative drew to a close. "That boy sure made fools of us! We were mighty gullible."

"We all swallowed his bait," Prine said. "We're lucky we're still alive. Y'know, this story makes a lot of things hang together. Like why Stuart was so quick to silence anyone who had come into contact with Priscilla's gang. He was afraid that they would tell the truth about him, and that would be the end of his scheme."

Thad was standing on the brink of the chasm, and he peered intently upward, his eyes squinted. The others walked up beside him. "What do you see, Thad?" asked Ballard.

Thad shook his head. "I'm not really sure. Take a look up there. Is that a light I see, some sort of opening?"

They all looked closely, eyes straining in the darkness. Suddenly Priscilla burst out in an excited voice: "He's right! There is an opening up there! Look!"

Then Prine saw it, along with the rest. A faint spot of light, circular, minuscule across the expanse, but definitely opening to the outside. It was so small that Prine could not even tell if it would accommodate a human form, and what was more, there was no way to know if any of the ledges that spiraled the vast chamber reached the opening. But still it was hope, no matter how remote.

"Prine, do you think—?"

"What else can we do, Ballard?"

Thad already had the lantern in his hand. "I'll go first. We'll have to move slow."

"Ballard, do you think you can stand the height?" Prine asked. "You say it gets to you after a while."

"So do hunger and thirst, Prine. I'd rather risk falling than starve to death in here."

Prine nodded. "Let's climb."

It seemed that years had passed since they had first moved out on the narrow ledge again to begin inching around toward the left, creeping snail-like toward the small opening high above. Thad was the leader. He first searched out the ledges ahead by the light of the lantern, then decided which way to go. Travel was more difficult for him than for the others, for he was encumbered by the lantern, and when he stepped he didn't have the advantage of having seen someone do it before him. But he moved along as quickly as could be expected.

Every muscle in every body ached. The rocks were dark and covered with slime, making them extremely hazardous, and what was more, no one could be sure that they would even reach the opening. They were still too far away for the lantern light to strike around it and show whether or not there was any sort of access to the exit. But the hole was growing ever-nearer.

Still, how long would it take for them to get there? And what if the hole was just out of reach? It could be merely a tantalizing opening to the outside just above them while they died a slow death, clinging to the rocks until they were so weakened that they slipped off into the dark lake far below.

Ballard's brow was coated with dank, nervous sweat, in spite of the coolness of the cavern. His hands trembled, and his legs seemed to be made of jelly. High places had never been comfortable for him, and as the group members progressed they were getting ever higher. His horrifying experience of dangling over the chasm while Stuart crushed his hands had not given him any more of a favorable feeling about this place.

Time crept on slowly. Ballard looked at the young girl before him. Her face was hardly visible, for the lantern light hardly reached back to them in spite of Thad's efforts to direct the beams, but from what he could see she was flushed, weary, bone-tired. He felt the same way. For a moment, despair filled him; death seemed to whisper in his ear. Ballard forced the feeling aside. He planned to live, not die.

Thad stopped ahead of them, the lantern held before him.

"What is it, Thad?" asked Prine. "There some sort of problem?"

Thad nodded his head slowly. "We got a gap up here, a big one. At least four feet with no ledge at all. I can see enough ledge on the other side of the gap to get us right below that opening. But this gap is a problem."

"Can we jump it, Thad?" Ballard called from the rear.

"I don't know . . . it looks like we'll have to try. I wish we had a rope—maybe I could tie some sort of safety line on the other side."

Prine frowned thoughtfully. "Maybe we can improvise something, Thad. Men, take off your gun belts. We can hook them together and make a line. Then Thad, you hold one end and jump across while I hold the other. If you should slip, maybe I can catch you."

"Then when I get to the other side, I can do the same for you, then together we can help the others," Thad said, completing the picture. "I can't say I relish the idea of playing mountain goat, but I can't see any other way."

"Here's my belt, Prine," said Ballard, handing his gun belt forward.

Prine removed his own gun belt; Thad did the same with his. When Prine linked them, he had a strong leather strap several yards in length. He handed one end to Thad.

"Strap that around your waist, Thad," Prine directed. "Make sure it's tight. I'll brace myself against this rock here—good, I think I'm set. Now you go ahead and jump when you feel like it." He paused. "And try to make it on the first try. Good luck."

Thad braced himself, quietly offering up a prayer. His leg muscles tensed, he crouched, waited, then leaped. The brief second he was in the air sent his stomach leaping inside of him; then his feet rested on solid rock and his hands grasped the cold and slimy stone on the other side of the gap.

"You made it, Thad!" exulted Prine. "You made it!" But his smile soon faded, for now it was his turn. Prine unsuccessfully tried to ignore the impulse to take one last glance down into the dark below him. As soon as he did it, he wished he hadn't.

"Leap away, Prine!" Thad shouted.

Prine flashed a deathly grin and jumped with all that was in him. He was surprised a moment later to find himself safely beside Thad on the other side. He looked at the young man and broke into a grin.

"I gave you a little help there, Prine," said Thad. "I yanked as you jumped. You almost landed on top of me!"

Prine laughed and slapped the young man on the shoulder. He examined the ledge on which they crouched. It was wider by far than that which they had previously passed over, and relative to the perils they had just faced, Prine felt as safe as an old maid sipping tea in her parlor.

But there were still Priscilla and Ballard to be brought over the opening. The girl, Prine thought, would be no problem, as light as she was. But Ballard might face difficulties.

They repeated the same procedure as before, this time with Priscilla. And almost before they had begun she was across, falling safely into Prine's arms, kissing him out of sheer joy to be alive. Thad wished jealously that he had been the one to whom she had leapt.

Thump!

Prine was shocked by the sudden tremor that shook the ledge. He turned and looked into the beaming face of John Ballard. The man had leaped unexpectedly, without help. And he had made it.

Prine was upset at the risk Ballard had taken.

"Why did you do a fool thing like that? Don't you know you could have fallen? Why didn't you wait until we were ready?"

"Shut up, Prine. Do you think for a minute that the three of you could have held me if I had slipped and fell? My weight would have pulled you right in after me."

Prine gave Ballard back his gun belt, then grinned. "Glad you made it. If you had fell into that lake the splash would have wet us all the way up here." Ballard didn't seem to appreciate the humor.

An hour later they had inched their way around to the side of the mountain where the opening was. From the flickering lantern light Prine could see the ledge that passed under the hole. It looked thin and weak, and far too low for them to reach the opening. But they would have to risk it, for there was nothing else they could do.

Within five minutes they stood almost directly below the opening, eyeing the thin ledge with doubt. Prine felt vague despair.

"There's only one thing to do, the way I see it," said Thad. "Me and Mr. Prine will go out on that ledge—we'll just have to hope it holds up—and he can boost me up to get into that hole. Then we can link the belts like we did before, and maybe I can pull everyone up."

Prine looked carefully at the ledge and the opening. "You're right, Thad. It's the only way I can see."

"No," said Priscilla. "That ledge might break with both of you. I'm lighter than either of you. I think I can climb up that wall to the opening. It doesn't look too steep. I'll crawl up in there, then Thad. Between us we can get the rest of you, using the belts like before. Don't argue with me about it—if you two go out on that ledge you'd likely wind up down in that water."

There was no arguing with a command like that, and before many more moments had passed the pretty blond was out on the thin ledge, linked belts strapped around her waist, Prine and Thad holding them at the other end. She looked carefully at the face of the rock leading up to the hole. Thad held the almost-empty lantern so she could see where her feet would rest, and then she began to climb.

Slowly upward she went, breathing hard, concentrating. It was excruciating work, but she made progress. She squelched her impulse to look down, and after several minutes of slow climbing her hands at last grasped the rim of the opening, and she pulled herself upward and into it.

She felt a burst of joy at the mere sight of the sky out the other side of the opening. For a time she could not take her eyes, and only with reluctance did she at last turn about in the narrow passage and call out to the others.

They returned her call. Within moments Thad was scaling the wall, Priscilla pulling with all her strength, looking down at him, and also past him into the vast blackness below him. Inch by inch he drew nearer, then he was up beside her, swinging the belts down to Prine.

"There won't be room for all of us up here in this little hole," said Thad. "I'll pull up Prine—you crawl on back toward the outside."

She heard the scuffling of Prine's feet against the rock wall as she moved on back in the tunnel, again drinking in the beauty of the sky. She could hear Thad groan as he fought with the straining belts. Prine pulled himself up into the tunnel beside Thad.

Ballard was alone in the chamber below, the lantern in his hand. He saw the chain of linked belts descend, and swallowed hard. He sat the lantern down as he did the best he could to secure himself. He began his climb.

Thad and Prine strained hard at the burden as Ballard's feet struggled to find a hold on the rough wall. Far slower than the others, he rose, his eyes nervously studying the taut belts that held his weight. He prayed they would hold.

His foot came down on an unseen patch of slime and he slipped. He stared up into the horrified faces of his partner and his son as suddenly he dropped, his weight making it impossible for them to support him completely. He struck the thin ledge, and it broke beneath him, sending a shower of rock falling down to the black lake below, the lantern making a magnificent arc of yellow light in the heart of the cavern before it was extinguished by the waters below.

Ballard was swinging out over the chasm once more, his life depending on the strength of the chain of belts and on the men who held it.

"Try to get a toehold!" cried Prine. "Start pulling yourself up!"

Straining, sweating, hurting—Ballard struggled up the

wall, sliding, slipping, occasionally finding a hold that would let him move up a few more inches. His hands clasped the belts that held him until his fingers were bleeding, and yet often it seemed he was losing the fight, sliding . . .

"Hang on, Ballard! Hang on!" Prine encouraged the hefty man, whose boots now found a firmer hold. They struck the tiny outcrop left by the falling ledge, and he pulled himself up several inches. Hope overcame panic.

Up—higher—he continued his climb, never taking his eyes away from those that looked down from above him. Higher . . . just a little more . . .

His hand clasped Prine's, then Thad's, and then he was up, safe, secure, and weeping like a baby. He threw his arms around the neck of his son, then his friend. Together they joined Priscilla at the end of the passage, then on through onto the grassy slope outside, beneath the sky, smelling the open air, the scent of rain coming from the west.

Down the slope they walked without a word, around toward the south, circling the mountain until they reached their horses, still tied near the main entrance of the mine. They mounted, Priscilla taking one of the packhorses, and began their descent, heading back down the mountain road, approaching the sleeping town of Jericho Creek.

"Prine?"

"Yes, Ballard?"

"Ain't it good to be alive!"

Prine grinned. "Amen to that, brother."

Prine sat beside Ballard on the boardwalk outside the only doctor's office in Jericho Creek. Prine's leg was in a bandage, making his pants leg buck out like that of an overstuffed scarecrow, and his ears were still ringing with the harsh scolding he had just received from the doctor for ignoring his pitchfork wound for as long as he had.

Thad walked out of the office, Priscilla beside him. Thad removed his hat long enough to show where the doctor had shaved his head along the scalp wound.

"You look like the injuns got to you, boy!" said Ballard.

"Fool doctor," muttered Prine. "I never met a sawbones yet fit for anything 'cept patching up horses." Ballard grinned on the sly to the two young folks behind him and Prine, and winked. Prine was sullen as a dejected child.

"I'm starving. Let's go find some food," said Thad. "I know we ain't got much money, but we got to eat sometime."

"I can tell you where you can find a lot of money, Thad," said Prine. "'Course, you might have a bit of trouble getting to it. But, if you're willing to try—"

"No thanks. I'll pass on that. I'll stick to farming from now on, if you don't mind."

The group moved down the dusty street toward the nearest cafe. It was a surprisingly nice place, and they ordered a hearty meal, every bit of which they devoured. Ballard had three huge mugs of strong coffee, then patted his middle and smiled.

"Now, folks, that's eating!" he said. "I don't plan to

touch another bite of jerky for a year or more. I think I'd rather starve."

Prine was still in a foul mood. "Looking at the size of your gut, it wouldn't hurt you to starve a little," he muttered.

It was two days before they left the little town at last, after their various wounds and bruises had healed a little. During that time they avoided any mention of their plans, for it was painful to think of being apart. Prine especially felt the pain, for he knew that he had nothing to return to but a life of riding and roaming, picking up work where he could find it.

So when at last the four of them sat mounted on the road, their smiles were few and forced. Ballard settled his chew of tobacco into his jaw and looked at Prine. Thad and Priscilla were off to the side, out of earshot, talking intently to each other.

"Prine, you know you're welcome to come with me back to the farm. There's more than enough work for all of us. Even Priscilla's going to ride back that way, maybe even stay a while."

Prine snorted. "From the looks of how she and Thad are getting along, I'd say she might stay permanent. She started out as Priscilla Tate, then we found out she was really Priscilla Stuart, and now it looks like she might wind up Priscilla Ballard. I'd say you'll lose your boy, Ballard."

"Just gaining a daughter-in-law," he said. "But you didn't answer my question. Are you coming with us?"

Prine looked down into the dust. "Ballard, there's no life for me but the one I'm living. And anyway, I couldn't abide having to stomp through manure on some farm."

Ballard looked at him sadly. "Suit yourself, Prine—but make sure you know that you're welcome anytime. I expect to see you again, real soon. All right?"

"You got a deal." Prine extended his hand, and the other took it. "Ol' Bob would have had a lot of tales to tell if he'd been around, wouldn't he!" Then Prine felt an overwhelming sadness, and turned away.

Priscilla and Thad came up to him, and their parting with Prine was difficult, especially for the girl. She hugged him, kissed him, and before she was through tears were in the eyes of both of them. Then they were on their way, Ballard and his group heading east, Prine sitting alone and watching them for a long time before he turned his horse west. He rode for several yards, then stopped. His eyes lifted to the massive peak of Jericho Mountain; then a smile played across his lips.

"Y'know," he said to himself, "maybe stomping through manure for a while wouldn't be bad at all."

He wheeled and headed at a gallop toward the band of riders, calling out to Ballard.

He saw the smile on the big man's face even before he was within a hundred yards of the waiting group.

THE TREASURE OF JERICHO MOUNTAIN
is the seventh Bantam Western by
CAMERON JUDD

And if you enjoyed this book, you will enjoy his eighth novel for Bantam . . .

MR. LITTLEJOHN

Here is an exciting preview of this new western novel, to be published in May, 1990. It will be available wherever Bantam Books are sold.

Turn the page for a sample of MR. LITTLE-JOHN by Cameron Judd.

Chapter 1

Winfred Priddy brought his traveling medicine show to Eldridge the week they buried and resurrected Dixie Trimble. When his big colorful wagon rolled into town, the hole where they had planted her still gaped like an open mouth and folks were rattling on about the awfulness of her premature burial one moment and the marvel of her rescue the next. It was a situation in which a clever man could make good money, for when people are excited, they're also gullible, and Priddy was the kind who could smell gullibility from miles away.

I was probably the only soul in Eldridge who hadn't been particularly surprised when Dixie was brought up alive out of her death hole, for Pa had always said the penultimate year of a decade brings unusual things. I had been on the watch for something peculiar since January.

Priddy's wagon rumbled up to Eldridge late in the day while I was in a house that didn't belong to me, looking for something that did. The house was that of Tim and Beulah Pearl, and their son, Mark, who was a year older than me and rotten as last Sunday's chicken. Mark had stolen a knife from me earlier in the week—the very knife Pa had left me before they hauled him off to Leavenworth three years ago—and I aimed to get it back. I was running a risk by poking through the Pearls' house, but that knife was important to me. Besides, the Pearls had left their back door open when they had gone off to ogle Dixie, who had replaced last fall's Dull Knife Comanche rampage as the chief talking material of all of Eldridge. I, for one, had no interest in eyeing Dixie any more than I had to, for to me she looked, as the saying goes, like death eating a cracker. But if Dixie was sickly, she at least was lucky on two scores: she had a loud moaning voice and a brave gravedigger. A lot of folks would have run off and kept quiet if they thought they had heard a moan come up from a new grave, but not this digger. He had just spaded Dixie right back up and run onto Rumbough Street shouting the news.

I poked about in Mark's room, in the chest of drawers and the wardrobe. So far no knife, just a half-smoked cigar and a picture under the mattress showing a lady in tights. That figured. Mark always was a nasty-minded fellow, with a mouth as dirty as a privy hole when his folks were out of earshot.

At last I found an old cigar box far back under Mark's bed, and inside it, my knife. I had just folded out the blades to make sure Mark hadn't broken any, which he hadn't, when I heard a rattle at the front door and Tim saying something about Dixie Trimble surely being guarded by heaven. I dashed quietly down the hall, cut into the kitchen, dropped and crabbed out toward the back porch through the still-open rear door, which I slid quietly shut just as Tim and his wife came in. I think Tim heard me, for he walked right over, and I barely had time to roll off the porch and down under it before he opened the door and came out, Mark right behind.

"Who's there?" Tim bellowed out in his big operatic voice.

I lay still and tried not to make noise. Tim and Mark walked around up above, the porch floorboards bending a little beneath them. It stunk where I was, for cats had peed down there. I hated to think what else I was lying in.

Beulah joined her menfolk on the porch. "What is it, sweetheart?"

"The breeze shook the door, I think," Tim answered. "I thought it was somebody running out."

Mark said, "Look yonder—medicine wagon coming."

Beulah replied, "So it is. Sure as shooting."

I twisted around a bit under the porch until I could see part of the wagon myself—a moving speck of color pulled by two big mules.

"I always like a good medicine show," Beulah said, "as long as they're decent in their entertainment."

"I don't care much for them," Tim returned. "Usually operated by scoundrels. Half or more of the ones we get here have just been run out of Wichita for one thing or another."

"Well, I still like them," Beulah reaffirmed.

She and Tim went back inside. Mark loitered around a bit longer, walking around right above me. After a minute something brown splattered the ground just off the edge of the porch and a few inches in front of my nose. Mark was chewing twist tobacco. A few minutes later the ugly brown cud thumped to the ground, and Mark went back inside. I waited another five minutes, then shimmied out and ran off. It was dusky dark, and the crickets were beginning to sing. The air smelled like suppertime.

Once I was well away from the Pearl house I relaxed and started walking slowly along, hands in my pockets. The day had been warm, but now was growing cool. All around me stretched Kansas flatlands, golden and majestic in the dimming light. Along the western horizon the sky was an indescribable hue, somewhere between the color of spun gold and that of the hair of a fair-complexioned newborn. I've heard people say that flatland sunsets aren't as worth seeing as those in the mountains, but I've seen both and I know which are best. I always felt that if a man could somehow drink a Kansas sunset, he'd never be thirsty again.

I sauntered onto Rumbough Street, Eldridge's main thoroughfare, and walked along beside the boardwalk. The medicine show wagon had preceded me and was parked across the street in a vacant lot down between Stansdale's Barber Shop and Rubideck's Restaurant. In front of the wagon a fellow in black pants and a white, balloon-sleeved shirt and arm garters was unhitching the mules, which were already grazing the spring grass at their hoofs. The man was stout, with legs like sawed-off telegraph poles. His clothes looked expensive if not neat, and he wore a tall hat that was so battered out of shape and so strangely cocked on his head that it looked like a mushroom growing out of his skull. He was talking as he worked, but all I could make out was a cuss word or two every now and then, which I assumed were directed at the mules. Then I realized there was a second man around the far side of the wagon. Of him I could see nothing but his legs, which were leaner than those of Mr. Mushroom Hat, and rooted down in tall yellow boots.

I leaned against a hitchpost, pulled a splinter from it, and picked my teeth while trying to watch the medicine show men without staring outright. The man on the other side of the wagon came around, and my brows quirked up in surprise. He was well over six feet tall and looked to have inherited his shoulders from an ox that didn't need them anymore. His hair was very long and yellow and hung about his head in the style popularized by the late Hickok. He wore a dirty blue shirt with cut-off sleeves, against which the muscles of his upper arms strained. His chest was broad and thick, his waist narrow. He looked like a strong man I had seen in a circus once—and then my eye fell on the wagon itself and I realized that a strong man was just what he was.

The writing on the wagon said: PRIDDY'S FAMILY ENTERTAINMENT & TONIC SUPPLY, ONLY TRANS-MISSISSIPPI SOURCE OF DR. DEMOREST'S RADI-

CAL PURGE. In smaller letters it continued: A FINE TONIC USED AND SANCTIONED BY THE ROYAL FAMILY OF BRITAIN AND PRESIDENT RUTHERFORD B. HAYES. Looking close, I could see even from where I stood that the president's name was a little bigger and darker than the other words, which let me know they had blocked it in over Ulysses S. Grant's name when he went out of office a couple of years back.

A little lower were the words: SEE SHERWOOD FOREST'S MR. J. LITTLEJOHN PERFORM FEETS OF AMAZING STRENGTH. Feets—that's the way they spelled it. WHOLESOME FAMILY ENTERTAINMENT AND HEALTHFUL EXHORTATION. EXTRA ATTRACTION: PHOTOGRAPHS TAKEN FOR MODEST FEE.

Though I was trying not to be obvious about watching the wagon, suddenly Mr. Mushroom Hat turned and eyed me, then motioned me to come. Curious, I headed over.

The wagon, closer up, appeared crude, nothing like fancy show wagons I'd seen before that were like fine mahogany furniture on wheels. This was just a glorified pine box built onto the bed of an old wagon. The paint work was uneven, patchy—not a professional job. The mules pulling the wagon looked fit only to be rations for some starving Indian family, and poor rations at that.

Priddy stuck out his hand. "Winfred Priddy," he said.

The hand was small as a woman's but calloused as a blacksmith's. "Pennington Malone," I returned.

Priddy, unlike the resurrected Dixie Trimble, had a descriptively inaccurate surname. Written across his face in pockmarks was the ugly and unerasable signature of childhood smallpox. His nose was bulbous and red, a meaty thing poking out over a dark waxy mustache. His eyes were too small for his head and his head was too small for his shoulders, and all in all he looked like somebody who ought to have bars in front of him. As for Mr. Littlejohn the strong man, he had gone to the back side of the wagon where I couldn't see him.

"Pleased. A question: Coming in, we passed a house with wagons, buggies, horses all around, people crowding in . . ."

"That would be the Trimble place," I cut in.

"What's the stir?"

I told him about Dixie. His eyes gleamed like cranked-up lantern wicks; he licked his lips beneath his mustache. I could tell he had heard wind of the story already, and was just trying to verify it.

"Fascinating!" he said. "Simply fascinating! A true premature burial! You are sure?"

"Yes, sir." I knew why he was doubtful. Fear of premature burial was a recurring obsession of the English speaking world these days. Reports of it came and went, ninety-five percent of them lies. I recalled having recently read in a newspaper about an 18-year-old Virginia girl who was thought to have died of neuralgia of the stomach. They had buried her despite one woman screeching that the girl was alive. The night after the burial the family got stirred up by the woman's talk, and they dug up the girl and found she had come awake in the coffin, torn out her hair, ripped up the coffin lining, and scratched her face to pieces before dying for real. Folks blamed the girl's doctor, who had given her a strong dose of morphine shortly before her supposed death—just like Dixie had taken before her own early planting. At that point the newspaper story had begun talking about some entirely vegetable miracle cough cure that contained nothing to put you to sleep and get you buried alive, and I had stopped reading.

I waved at the wagon. "When does the show begin?"

"Tomorrow night, at dark," Priddy said. "A good show, fit for the family." He looked me up and down, eyeing my threadbare clothes. "You have family, Mr. Malone?"

"Call me Penn. My only family is my pa, and he's in the state penitentiary at Leavenworth. He used to write me letters sometimes, but now he quit. He's a common thief.

I don't know where my mother is. She ran off with a drummer when I was five years old, and took my sister with her. I live with the local wagonmaker and his wife, but they had a son of their own who died fifteen years ago and they don't find me a fit replacement. I work for the old man. Other than that I'm alone in this old world."

I told him all that because I figured it would soften the heart of the most petrified sinner; I hoped to make Priddy feel sorry for me and give me a coin or two for my woes. But all I got was a cold, flat stare. Maybe Priddy took it all for a lie, which it wasn't, or more likely he just didn't care.

"This Trimble girl—what kind of health is she in now?"

"Terrible. But she's always that way, and sort of seems to enjoy it. She writes poems all about it."

"Poems . . . good ones?"

"Depends on what you like."

"Would she read them from a stage, perhaps? You think she could write one about her experience—a rescue-from-the-bowels-of-the-earth sort of thing?"

I shrugged. "Knowing Dixie and the shape she stays in, she probably knows more about bowel pains than the bowels of the earth. But you could ask her."

"That I shall."

I understood him now: he figured to hire her for his show here. I couldn't fault the idea; a living cadaver such as Dixie would draw plenty of attention.

"Can I meet Mr. Littlejohn?" I asked. The strong man was still at the backside of the wagon, fiddling with something. I wanted to see him closer up.

"Come to the show," Priddy said as he walked away.

I told Old Halley and Mrs. Halley about the medicine show while we ate supper, but they didn't seem interested. They seldom were interested in anything I had to say. But when I told them the show might feature Dixie, they did perk up a bit.

After supper I headed to my room, which was just a

shed built at the rear and onto the side of Halley's Wagon Works. The Halleys had a spare room in their house, which stood directly behind the wagon works, but that had been their late son's room and they didn't let me use it. I never had figured out why the old couple had ever agreed to keep me in the first place. As best I could tell, after Pa was put away, the Presbyterian preacher had played on Old Halley's conscience about my pitiable condition until the old man took me out of a combination of guilt and a probable desire for cheap labor in the wagon shop.

I told Pa in my letters how they treated me, but it never drew any response from him. The few letters he sent back from the penitentiary never acknowledged my troubles at all. After awhile I began to feel like an orphan. Pa's letters came less often and finally stopped. By then it had hardly seemed to matter, for I no longer believed he cared anything about me.

It had come to me a few months ago that I would have no life at all unless I built it myself. I began saving my meager wages from Old Halley and making plans to leave when I had enough to hold me over for awhile. I just hoped Old Halley wouldn't get into a rage with me—those were becoming more common now—and wallop me to death with a wagon spoke or something before I had a chance to run off.

Early the next morning, when the smell of dawn still hung in the air like a perfume scent, I finally saw Mr. Littlejohn up close. I was asleep on my bunk when I heard a stirring in the alley outside. I rose, slipped on my shirt and pants and pulled galluses over my shoulders. I went to the door and cracked it open.

The strong man was out there, washing his face in a bucket sitting atop an upside-down rain barrel. He must have come back into the alley for some privacy. He was no more than fifteen feet away, but was sideways to me and apparently hadn't heard me open the door, for he continued washing without looking up. His galluses hung down past his knees, but his grimy blue shirt was still on.

When he was finished, he ran his wet hands through his long hair and shook his head like a wet-eared dog, then started unbuttoning the shirt.

I must have made a noise, for he wheeled so fast it made me jump. He did two peculiar things then. First, he lunged toward me a little like he was going to grab me. It seemed an instinctive move like a fighter would make. Then he straightened, pulled his shirt back together as fast as he could, as if he was embarrassed, and started buttoning it up.

"Good morning. Didn't mean to disturb you," I said.

Unspeaking, he picked up the bucket, tossed out the water, turned his back on me and walked off, the bucket swinging and his long hair dripping down on his shoulders.

Chapter 2

I saw the strong man next about an hour after a typically joyless breakfast with the Halleys. I had just left the house when I heard the boom of a drum echoing down the street. I headed for the sound; lots of other curious folks were doing the same.

Mr. Littlejohn was the drummer. He stood on a stage that was folded out from the side of the wagon. It was wide as the wagon itself and rested on big pole supports that fit neatly in slots when it was folded up for travel. With the stage down, the wagon didn't look so crude. There was even a wrinkled red curtain hanging at the back.

Winfred Priddy stood to the side of the stage at a little podium like those you see in country churches. He looked as pompous as a freshly fed bishop.

"Ladies and gentlemen!" he boomed out. "I am Winfred Coleman Priddy, showman of the West, friend of the family, conveyor of health, and for a brief day or two, one of your populace. I join you with my companion, the likes of which, I assure you, you have never seen before!"

At this he gestured at the strong man, who deftly spun his drumsticks between his cigar-sized fingers and did a practiced bow. Though Mr. Littlejohn was smiling, it reminded me of a smile I had once seen a mischievous undertaker put on a corpse: it just wasn't heartfelt. Mr. Littlejohn obviously had become uncomfortable the moment Priddy directed attention to him.

"Have you ever seen such a figure? Not since the days of old has there been a giant so large or a human so powerful!" The description was an exaggeration; Mr. Littlejohn was big, but no giant, though his muscled form was something to see.

"Friends, this modern-day Hercules is a living miracle, made what he is by equal portions of good stock, exercise, healthful eating, and proper medicinal intake. Mr. Littlejohn is an authentic descendent of the famed companion of Sherwood Forest's Robin Hood. He is a muscled marvel, a pinnacle of power, here to demonstrate the astounding potential for strength and vitality built by the creator into the human creature!"

Here the strong man did an impressive drum roll that crescendoed up to a final bang. I had the impression that folks were supposed to applaud at that point in gratitude for the good fortune Priddy was bringing them, but nobody made a sound. Everybody had seen medicine shows before, and were waiting for him to get to the part about the tonic he was hawking.

Which he promptly did: "And, my friends, we will present to you a product available nowhere else this side of the Mississippi, one that, when used as prescribed by its inventor, Dr. Cooper Demorest of Baltimore, can provide to you the benefits of a health that age cannot diminish and a vitality that the chilly Kansas wind cannot blast away." Here Priddy dropped his voice so dramatically low it seemed to rumble along the ground. "Dr. Demorest's Radical Purge is a purifying tonic made specifically for the American of the plains. Dr. Demorest is a physician who lost three of his own children to the plagues peculiar to these flat, windswept lands. As he laid the third away to eternal rest, he made a vow. Back to Baltimore I will go and develop a formula to preserve these delicate lives, so easily snuffed away! And this he did . . . and to me alone he has entrusted sales of this potion, this protector and strengthener of life's sweet breath.

"Where does the fountain of life lie, my friends? In the liver! Why else would this organ have the name it does?" He paused to let us think that over; I had to admit it sort of made sense. "Dr. Demorest's formula works through the natural purging of the liver . . . and this without narcotics or morphia . . ."

The crowd was growing restless now. Somebody yelled: "If Dr. Demorest is so hot for his purge, why ain't he out selling it himself?"

"A good question, my skeptical friend! The doctor remains in Baltimore, developing Dr. Demorest's Stomach Bitters, a product superior to that of any competitor. When that is done he will join me in bringing that new product to the good people of the West."

"You going to put on a show or not?" another shouted.

"Indeed. Tonight at dark. Free of charge, and of highest quality."

"How much alcohol in that tonic?" somebody else yelled, drawing laughter.

"Only the minimal amount required by an elixer," Priddy promptly shot back. "Dr. Demorest's purpose is the purging, not the pickling, of the liver." That drew another laugh. He probably used that line everywhere he went.

I had been watching the strong man. He was still smiling at the crowd, but still only on the outside. Beneath his pasted-on grin there was something restless and maybe sad, and his eyes, as they darted across the crowd, were fast and nervous as a snake-cornered rabbit's.

I turned around and slipped off toward the wagon shop. Old Halley had decided to keep it closed today, as he did many Fridays since he had started getting up in years, but had told me to straighten it up and sweep it out. As I walked away I heard Priddy saying something about a surprise guest at tonight's show, and knew he had gotten to Dixie Trimble sometime last night.

Well, she'd make a crowd-pleasing addition, I figured,

though they'd probably have to prop her up on a frame to show her off.

When I finished sweeping, the morning was gone. I went back to my room and dug out some old crackers and cheese from the chest beneath my bunk. Mrs. Halley had been feeling poorly after breakfast and had gone back to bed for a nap, and naps for her lasted two thirds of a day. I wasn't allowed to dig around in her kitchen and thus couldn't make lunch myself—and I sure wouldn't ask Old Halley to fix me something. I kept a little cache of food for just such occasions.

After I ate I went to the well, cranked down a bucket and brought it up brimming with cold water. I put away three dipperfuls, poured out the bucket, then turned and almost ran square into Ivar Norris, who had crept up silently.

He laughed when I jumped back. I backed up too hard against the mouth of the well, teetered there for a minute, then pulled back up.

"Ivar, I almost fell in!" Ivar merely laughed again. He sneaked as good as an Indian and loved to play this sort of trick on people.

"Calm down, Penn. I'd have caught you," he said. "I came to get you to do me a favor."

"Don't know why I'd do a favor for somebody who'd try to scare me down a well."

"Hush and listen: somebody said you were a friend of that medicine show barker. Said you were visiting with him right after he came in."

"I talked to him a bit. What's your interest?"

Ivar gave me a surreptitious look. "That Littlejohn fellow—Gene Garfield wants to fight him."

Gene was the biggest man in Eldridge, a rawboned mountain of gristle and scars who had gone all the way through the worst of the Civil War and had come out still thirsty for blood. He did saddlework for his living, but made good money on the side by boxing in saloons and back alleys all over Kansas. It was a popular sport, and Gene was good at it, so good he had nearly killed two opponents in Wichita and been told never to return.

"Why doesn't Gene ask him?" I asked.

"You think anybody would agree to fight if he laid eyes on Gene first? I figure that if you know those folks already, you're the best one to ask."

I thought about it a moment, then said I would do it—for fifty cents.

Ivar's eyes narrowed. "That's robbery, Penn."

I smiled and said, "It runs in my family."

He scowled at me and dug into his pocket.

ABOUT THE AUTHOR

I was born in 1956 in Tennessee, the state in which I have lived all my life. I wrote my first western at age twenty-two; since then four others have been published, and now I am writing exclusively for Bantam.

My interest in the American West is just part of a broader interest in the frontier. I am fascinated by the vast westward expanses on the other side of the Mississippi, but I am equally intrigued by the original American West: the area west of the Appalachians and east of the Mississippi. I hope someday to write fiction set in that older frontier at the time of its settlement, in addition to traditional westerns.

My interest in westerns was sparked in early childhood by television, movies, and books. I love both the fact of the West and the myth of the West; both aspects have a valid place in popular fiction, in my view.

I received an undergraduate degree in English and journalism, plus teaching accreditation in English and history, from Tennessee Technological University in 1979. Since that time I have been a journalist by profession, both as a writer and editor. Today I am managing editor of the daily newspaper in Greeneville, Tennessee, one of the state's most historic towns. Greeneville is the seat of the county that contributed one of America's original frontier heroes to the world—Davy Crockett. Greeneville was also the hometown of President Andrew Johnson and was for several years the capital of the Lost State of Franklin—an eighteenth-century political experiment that came close to achieving statehood.

I live in rural Greene County with my wife, Rhonda, and children, Matthew and Laura and Bonnie (as of the time of this book's publication).

ELMER KELTON

THE MAN WHO
RODE MIDNIGHT

☐ 27713 **$3.50**

Bantam is pleased to offer these exciting Western adventures by ELMER KELTON, one of the great Western storytellers with a special talent for capturing the fiercely independent spirit of the West:

☐ 25658	**AFTER THE BUGLES**	$2.95
☐ 27351	**HORSEHEAD CROSSING**	$2.95
☐ 27119	**LLANO RIVER**	$2.95
☐ 27218	**MANHUNTERS**	$2.95
☐ 27620	**HANGING JUDGE**	$2.95
☐ 27467	**WAGONTONGUE**	$2.95
☐ 25629	**BOWIE'S MINE**	$2.95
☐ 26999	**MASSACRE AT GOLIAD**	$2.95
☐ 25651	**EYES OF THE HAWK**	$2.95
☐ 26042	**JOE PEPPER**	$2.95